Best Stories
from the
Indian Classics

In this selection of stories from the classics of Sanskrit fiction, Professor Naravane offers fascinating glimpses of life in ancient India. Retold in modern English and presented in a lively, fluent style, these stories are marked by an amazing diversity of atmosphere, situation, attitudes and characterization. They reveal the continuity of Indian tradition through the centuries, and convey the unique, distinctive flavour of Indian life and culture.

VISHWANATH S. NARVANE was born in Allahabad. He did his Ph.D. from Allahabad University and was on the faculty of that university for two decades. Later he went on lecture tours in many countries and was a Visiting Professor at several colleges and universities in the USA. Besides philosophy and religion, he taught courses in Indian history, art and literature. He has published more than a dozen books including *Modern Indian Thought, The Elephant and the Lotus* (a collection of essays with a highly appreciative Foreword by Professor A. L. Basham) and monographs on Rabindranath Tagore, Anand Coomaraswamy, Munshi Premchand, Sarojini Naidu and Sarat Chandra Chatterji.

Best Stories
from the
Indian Classics

SELECTED AND RETOLD BY

V. S. Naravane

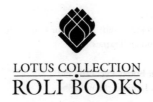

LOTUS COLLECTION
ROLI BOOKS

Lotus Collection

First published in 1994
Fourth impression 2005
The Lotus Collection
An imprint of
Roli Books Pvt. Ltd.
M-75, G.K. II Market
New Delhi 110 048
Phones: ++91 (11) 2921 2271, 2921 2782
2921 0886, Fax: ++91 (11) 2921 7185
E-mail: roli@vsnl.com; Website: rolibooks.com
Also at
Bangalore, Varanasi, Jaipur and the Netherlands

Cover design: Sneha Pamneja
Cover photo: Courtesy Martand Singh, Rta Kapur Chishti and Rahul Jain, from
their book 'Handcrafted Indian Textiles'.

Typeset in Galliard by Roli Books Pvt. Ltd. and
printed at Gopsons Papers Limited, New Delhi.

'Centuries before Kalidasa and Valmiki were heard of outside India, Indian stories were told and retold in distant corners of Asia and Europe. From Boccacio to Chaucer and Shakespeare, right down to Le Sage, La Fontaine and Voltaire—all were influenced by these tales!

' The pure-minded sage, the distraught poet, the self-effacing reformer, the restless wanderer: characters such as these who cmerge from the stories are intensely real. There is the credulous peasant, the voluble astrologer, the rapacious priest, the servile courtier, the pedantic scholar—each one of them has a story to relate and a lesson to teach. It is heartening to know that a thousand years ago, the Indian barber was as garrulous as he is today, and that, predictably, the grocer's weights were not always accurate!'

CONTENTS

PREFACE

India is the original home of
fiction. It was fiction, rather than poetry or drama, which first put India
on the literary map of the world. Centuries before Kalidasa and Valmiki
were heard of outside India, stories of Indian origin were told and
retold in distant corners of Asia and Europe. They were picked up by
the Persians and the Arabs, who passed them on to the Turks. From
the markets of Constantinople this precious, though invisible,
merchandize was forwarded to Venice and Naples. Many a tale in the
Decameron owes its central idea to some episode in the *Jatakas* or the

Kathasaritsagara. From Boccacio to Chaucer, from Chaucer to Cervantes and Shakespeare, right down to Le Sage, La Fontaine and Voltaire—what a wonderful journey in time and space!

Ancient Indian fiction offers a diversity of theme, atmosphere and situation unequalled in world literature. Some of the stories are saturated with the spirit of piety and religious devotion; others reveal a refreshingly secular and objective attitude to life. Some are products of pure fancy, and show an insatiable love of invention for its own sake; others are realistic, and their shrewd practicalism provides a healthy corrective to the mystical excesses of the Indian consciousness. Some are profound, weighty, deep; others compensate by their vigour, their uninhibited freedom. Some are soft and delicate like the pulp of ripe pears; others are sharp like pineapples—their texture is far from tender, but the flavour is full bodied.

As we read these tales from ancient India, we are struck by the amazing continuity of Indian life and culture across the centuries. They show us how little India has changed in spite of mighty political upheavals, the rise and fall of empires, the mingling of races, the clash of sects and religions. In ancient times India was as much a land of contrasts as it is today: wealth and want, grandeur and simplicity, transparent sincerity and unashamed chicanery, saintliness and cynicism, refinement and crudeness.

The men and women who emerge from these stories are intensely real to us. There is the pure-minded sage, the detached philosopher, the distraught poet, the self-effacing reformer, the restless wanderer. There is the blushing bride, the tireless housewife, the miserable widow. There is the credulous peasant, the voluble astrologer, the rapacious priest, the pompous grandee, the servile courtier, the pedantic scholar. It would appear that a thousand years ago the Indian barber was as garrulous as he is now; and it is very much to be feared that then, as now, the grocer's weights were not always accurate.

In the pages that follow I invite readers to join a series of expeditions into this exciting realm of fact and fancy. We cannot hope to explore more than a small portion of this vast continent. But we shall assuredly climb a few imposing peaks, step into some fertile valleys, tramp the lanes of a few populous cities and sail upon a number of interesting rivers. Now and again we might drift into regions where the path is rugged, the air oppressive and the water unpalatable. But these will be followed by healthier climes where the breeze will allay our fatigue and the fragrance of flowers will soothe our nerves.

From some of these excursions we shall return wiser, though a trifle sadder. Others will bring us unmixed delight. But whatever the outcome, I feel sure that the journeying itself will not be tiresome.

19 March 1994   V. S. NARAVANE
Allahabad

THE PANCHATANTRA

*T*here are several versions of the
Panchatantra. *They all go back to a common original, which is irrevocably
lost. This original version* perhaps *belongs to Kashmir; it is* possible *that
the stories were composed in their present form some time between the second
and the fourth centuries, and the author was* probably *Vishnusharman.
That is all that the scholars can tell us!*

*Centuries ago the Panchatantra stories had already passed into
universal currency. Age after age, and in every part of the world, they
have brought delight to old and young alike. What is the secret of this*

unrivalled popularity? The answer is that no other book in the world contains so much practical wisdom, offered in such a palatable form, and expressed with such subtle understanding of the aesthetic as well as the psychological requirements of human nature.

The Panchatantra *is not meant for ascetics. It presumes that all-round happiness, here and now, is the central aim of life. But happiness is not a fruit that is easily plucked. You have to struggle for it. Unflagging effort, coupled with wit and resourcefulness, leads to success: such is the theme of the* Panchatantra. *The importance of wealth and powerful friends is not overlooked. In fact the* Panchatantra *may justly be described as the first treatise ever written on 'How to Win Friends and Influence People'. Nevertheless, you cannot pull off anything really decisive merely with the help of money or friends in high office. In the last resort it is a combination of ingenuity and unremitting toil that counts.*

Life, as actually lived, is not always edifying. The Panchatantra *faces this fact squarely. As Sthirajivi, Chief Counsellor to the king of Crows, points out, the world is full of unscrupulous people; and piety does not always protect us from them. Good deeds are seldom appreciated. Ingratitude dogs our footsteps. We are surrounded by chicanery, artifice and pretence. The* Panchatantra *therefore recommends shrewdness, realism and freedom from excessive sentimentality.*

And yet, although it portrays the seamy side of life, the Panchatantra *does not preach cynicism. On the contrary, the path of honesty is declared to be the most proper and dependable course. As the frog Gangadatta says: 'A muddy garment soils every other object with which the wearer comes into contact. Likewise, when one virtue is abandoned all others gradually desert us.'*

But the Panchatantra *shows us that a virtuous man need not be a simpleton, and that our actions can be reasonably meritorious without being tiresome!*

THE
PANCHATANTRA

In the southern country there
once ruled a great king named Amarashakti. Many monarchs
recognized his overlordship and bowed before his might. King
Amarashakti was not merely powerful; he was also wise, learned and
intelligent. He was well-versed in all the arts and familiar with all the
principles of practical conduct.

Blessed with so much renown, wealth, ability and virtue the king
should have considered himself a very happy man. But he had,
unfortunately, one great source of sorrow. All his three sons were utter
imbeciles.

For a long time the king endured his anxiety and disappointment, hoping that in course of time the princes would overcome their stupidity. At last one day he summoned his advisers and said, 'Gentlemen, as you all know, my sons are supreme idiots. They have neither commonsense nor discernment. Between them and education there seems to be a rooted hostility. When I see them, my kingdom no longer brings me any joy. It has been said that sons are of three kinds—those not yet born, those that are dead and those that are fools. Well, among these the unborn and the dead are very much to be preferred. They may cause grief for a limited period, but fools bring us sorrow throughout life. To beget a son who turns out to be a dunce is like buying a cow who neither bears a calf nor yields milk. I beseech you, gentlemen, to ponder over my problem. You must think of some method of awakening in my sons a spark of intelligence.'

The advisers suggested different solutions, but they carried no conviction to the king. The sciences and the arts recommended by them for the princes, as a necessary preparation for the awakening of intelligence, would have demanded years and years of study. The king was on the verge of despair, but one of the advisers held out hope. He said, 'Your Majesty, life is short and the sciences involve much time. What we need is some kind of a precis containing, so to say, the essence of all wisdom and intelligence. We must pick out the fundamental facts and separate them from the subsidiaries, as swans extract pure milk from a mixture of milk and water. Now, there is only one man capable of preparing such an epitome of wisdom. That man is Vishnusharman. Let us entrust the princes to his care. I am sure he will make them intelligent.'

Accordingly the king sent for Vishnusharman. When he arrived, the king said, 'Sir, you will be doing me a great favour by teaching my sons the art of practical life. In return you shall have the revenue of a hundred villages.' The Brahmin replied, 'Listen, Oh King! I am

not in the habit of selling learning for monetary gain. Besides, I have
no use for money. I have attained a ripe old age and objects of desire
no longer hold out a charm for me. So let us forget about the revenue
from a hundred villages. But I shall be happy to take charge of your
sons. And if I do not make them, within a period of six months, masters
of the art of intelligent living, I shall give up my own name.'

The king was relieved to hear Vishnusharman's categorical
promise. The boys were handed over to him and he took them home.
There he taught them the five books of stories in which the essence
of worldly wisdom was compressed. Having learned these stories the
princes became thoroughly conversant with all the arts of life. At the
end of six months they returned to the Palace cured of their imbecility,
much to the delight of their royal father.

BOOK ONE

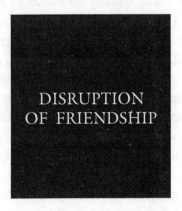

DISRUPTION
OF FRIENDSHIP

Once there was a city called Mahilaropya. Its buildings were magnificent; their walls and spires rose into the sky like the mighty Himalayas. In this city, populous and overflowing with wealth, there lived a merchant named Vardhamana. He was a virtuous man and, through hard work, accumulated a vast fortune. Once, pondering over his possessions, he reflected: 'Though money is abundant, it should be increased. What is unearned should be earned, what is earned should be preserved; what is preserved should be expanded; what is expanded should be profitably invested. I must therefore set out and strive to multiply my wealth.'

And so, collecting a large stock of merchandize, he said farewell to his parents and took the road to Mathura. He was accompanied by trusted servants, and his cart was drawn by two powerful bulls named Nandaka and Sanjivaka. By and by the merchant and his followers reached a dense forest. It was cool and shady, full of restful caves and thickets, abounding in bubbling streams. But it was also the haunt of tigers, bears and other ferocious animals. While they were passing through this forest, the bull Sanjivaka slipped at a muddy spot and sank upon the ground. Overcome by the weight of the wagon, he was unable to rise and suffered great pain. The merchant halted for five nights, but when the poor bull did not recover he left him in charge of servants with a supply of fodder and proceeded towards his destination. In a day or two the servants, scared by the perils that lurked in the forest, abandoned Sanjivaka and journeyed to Mathura. They made a false report to their master. 'Poor Sanjivaka died,' they said. 'So we performed the last rites and came away. What a pity! He was such a fine animal.'

Meanwhile Sanjivaka managed to raise himself up and hobbled to the banks of the Yamuna. There he browsed on the young shoots of grass and drank his fill from the river. Within a few days he grew plump and vigorous. Full of energy, and high-humped like Nandi, the bull of Lord Siva, he romped about with supreme unconcern.

One day a lion named Pingalaka came to the Yamuna's banks and heard the bull bellowing loudly. The sound was unlike anything he had ever heard, and the lion was sorely troubled. Concealing his panic he lay down under a mighty banyan tree and sent for all his retainers. Pingalaka had never experienced any restraint; he had ruled with absolute power and was a stranger to caution and fear alike. He was a lion, and a lion needs no anointing. Nature herself had crowned him king. But now for the first time he was stricken with fear.

Among the innumerable animals in Pingalaka's train, there were two jackals named Karataka and Damanaka. They were sons of former counsellors but were at that time out of employment. Damanaka detected a change in the king's expression and guessed that something was amiss. 'My dear Karataka,' he said to his friend, 'just look at our master. Why does he suddenly look so shaken up?' Karataka said, 'Why should we meddle? Wise people keep to their own affairs. The two of us pick up enough out of the master's leavings. Let's be content.'

But Damanaka was not satisfied. 'After all,' he said, 'food is not everything. We must strive for distinction. Even a crow can fill his belly so long as he has a beak. Dogs wag their tails and roll at their masters' feet for scraps of food. But elephants have so much self-esteem that they have to be coaxed into eating.'

'Anyway,' said Karataka, 'we are out of jobs. We have no standing at court. So what can we do?'

'Don't be such a pessimist, my dear fellow. The holder of a job may be fired, and a jobless fellow may acquire a position of trust if he has real worth. I know how to make myself useful. I have carefully studied Vyasa's account of how clever people behave at the court. I understand the duties of a shrewd functionary. I know that through sheer physical proximity I can obtain royal favour; for kings, like maidens and creepers, cling to their nearest neighbours. I know when to keep silent and when to answer.'

Karataka said, 'Well, if you have made up your mind, by all means go and speak to the king. I wish you luck.' And so Damanaka went to meet Pingalaka. When the king saw him approach, he said to the guard, 'Enough of your formalities. Admit him without ceremony. Damanaka is an old acquaintance and a counsellor's son.' So the jackal entered the inner enclosure and respectfully sat down at the place indicated to him. The king greeted him with his formidable right paw and said, 'It is ages since you were last seen. I do hope you have been in good health.' Damanaka said, 'Sir, we are the ancestral servants of

your dynasty. In times of need we come forward. Even a straw may
serve a king to scratch an ear or to pick a tooth. But when speech and
action are required the king has to count upon his loyal followers. I
may be a mere jackal but you will not despise me for that. Silk comes
from worms, gold from stones, gems from hoods of snakes, and the
lotus thrives in mud.'

'My good fellow, have I ever despised you? You are an old
retainer. Now tell me what has brought you here.'

'Your Majesty set out to enjoy a drink at the Yamuna. Why did
you suddenly return and camp under this tree?'

'For no particular reason, my friend.'

'Of course, if it is a state secret I shall not say another word. A
king has to be circumspect.'

At this Pingalaka reflected: 'The fellow seems trustworthy. One
must share one's fears with an honest servant or a faithful friend. I
think I should take him into confidence.' And so, lowering his voice,
he asked, 'Damanaka, did you hear a peculiar sound coming from the
bank of the river?'

'Yes, master, I did. But what of it?'

'1 am thinking of leaving this forest on account of this strange
voice. I think some prodigious creature has come here. The place is
no longer safe.'

'What! Is Your Majesty frightened by a mere voice? All kinds of
sounds are heard here. We hear the thunder of clouds, the wind
rustling among the reeds, drums, noisy carts, temple-bells and so many
other noises. You cannot abruptly leave this forest which was won by
your ancestors and has been in the family estate for generations. Remain
on the spot until I find out what sort of a creature he is.'

When Damanaka was gone, Pingalaka repented his haste. 'I think
it was a mistake,' he thought, 'to have trusted him to the point of
revealing my fears. The fellow has been out of job for some time, and

unemployment breeds bitterness. He may betray me to my new enemy.' Meanwhile Damanaka followed the direction of the sound and came close to the bull, who was grunting through sheer contentment. 'Well, well,' chuckled Damanaka, 'so it is nothing more dangerous than a bull. This is lucky for me. I can now have the king in my power by feeding his fears. A man restored to health no longer needs a drug; and a king relieved of worry no longer needs a counsellor.' So when he returned to Pingalaka he pulled a long face and looked very grim. 'I managed to see the creature,' he said with a dubious expression.

'Really? Are you telling me the truth?'

'How could I dare to make a false report? Besides, it is a sin to lie to the king. Sages have declared that the king is greater than all the Gods to his subjects. The Gods pay for good or ill after a lifetime. But the king pays at once.'

'All right, all right, I suppose you did really see him. Is he really very formidable?'

'Why waste words? Formidable or not, I shall somehow manage to bring him into your presence.'

The lion was happy, and Damanaka went back to the river bank. Approaching Sanjivaka he said, with a great show of anger, 'Come here, you impudent bull. How dare you keep up this stupid bellowing? My master Pingalaka is annoyed with you.' Sanjivaka asked, 'My friend, who is this Pingalaka?'

'What! You don't know who my master is? Just wait, you will soon learn. My master lives under a banyan tree not far from here. He is a mighty lion, lord over all life.'

The very mention of a lion threw Sanjivaka into panic. He considered himself as good as dead. When he recovered speech, he pleaded with the jackal to intercede with his master on his behalf, so that a safe-conduct may be granted to him. Damanaka promised to try and went back to Pingalaka. 'Oh master,' he said, 'that creature is

not an ordinary bull. He has served as the vehicle of Siva himself. And
he claims that this forest has been given to him as a playground.'

'Alas! My worst fears have come true,' said the lion. 'Only
through the special favour of the Gods can creatures wander in the
forest thundering like that. Now what shall we do?'

'Don't worry, Sir,' said Damanaka. 'I have told the bull that you
are the vehicle of Parvati and that the forest is your domain as well as
his. Furthermore, I. have invited him as a guest. He will come and
befriend you. But he has asked for a safe-conduct. It is for you to judge
whether you should grant it.'

Pingalaka was delighted. 'Excellent, my dear fellow,' he said, 'that
was most intelligent of you. Of course I grant him a safe-conduct. You
must now bring him here as quickly as possible; but remember, he
too has to bind himself by oath not to do me harm.' So Damanaka
went back once again to Sanjivaka and said, 'Well, I have persuaded
my master to grant you a safe-conduct. You may come with me without
anxiety. But you have to act in agreement with me. And don't take
on airs. By and by we shall both enjoy wealth and power. I am a king's
retainer; and you must know that it does not pay to behave haughtily
towards royal retainers. Don't forget the story of the merchant
Vajradanta.'

'1 have never heard of the merchant Vajradanta', said Sanjivaka.
'What happened to him?'

'I shall tell you,' said Damanaka, and he related this story.

THE SERVANT'S
REVENGE

In a certain prosperous city there once lived a merchant named Vajradanta. He had a vast private business and also handled the royal finances. He was so clever that he managed to gain popularity at the court as well as with the common people. He had a knack of reconciling contrary interests and making himself indispensable to all parties.

Now one day the merchant gave a big feast to celebrate his daughter's wedding. He invited the king, the ministers and all the prominent citizens. When the banquet was over, he regaled them with

gifts and escorted the king back to the palace. When the party reached
the palace, the merchant discovered one of the king's domestics, a man
called Vrishabha, comfortably seated at a prominent place. He hastened
to catch hold of the impudent fellow and drove him out of the hall.
From that moment Vrishabha vowed vengeance against the merchant.
He was restless all the time and sought an opportunity to harm the
man who had humiliated him.

Early one morning, as the king lay half awake, Vrishabha was
sweeping the room. When he approached the king's bed he muttered,
'What a shameless fellow this merchant is! How dare he make love to
the queen!' The king was startled. He jumped out of bed and said,
'What nonsense have you been talking, Vrishabha? What is all this about
the queen and Vajradanta?'

Pretending to be confused, Vrishabha said, 'Forgive me, Your
Majesty. I was awake all night and so I am feeling very drowsy. I do
not know what I said. Please give no thought to the matter.'

But the king's suspicions were aroused. He reflected: 'After all,
such a remark cannot be altogether accidental. This man has free
entrance to my palace. Vajradanta, too, comes and goes at his will.
Perhaps the servant has actually seen him caressing my queen. Who
can be sure of a woman's faithfulness?' The more he pondered the
more convinced he became that Vrishabha had blurted out the truth.
He withdrew his favour from Vajradanta and no longer invited him
to the court. The merchant was baffled by the king's sudden
indifference. One day, however, Vrishabha mocked him in the presence
of other servants. 'Be careful, my friends,' he said. 'This merchant is
one of the king's great favourites. He can arrest anyone he wants. Don't
offend him, otherwise he will box your ears as he boxed mine.' And
with these words he laughed loudly.

The mystery now became clear to Vajradanta. He reflected: 'So,
it was Vrishabha's doing. Well, I was foolish to have offended him. A

servant, however base he may be, can always get his vanity satisfied if he is sufficiently close to the monarch.' He went home in deep dejection and pondered how he might regain the king's favour. At last he apologized to the servant and presented him with two garments of silk. Vrishabha's vanity was flattered. 'All right, I forgive you,' he said. 'I shall soon restore you to the king's favour.'

Next morning Vrishabha again pretended to be drowsy while he was sweeping the king's bedchamber. 'How intelligent our king is,' he muttered. 'While taking his bath he eats cucumbers.' The king was amazed when he heard this remark. 'What is all this piffle, Vrishabha?' he said with great annoyance. 'It is only because you have served me for many years that I am sparing you. Otherwise such a remark would have cost you your life. Have you ever seen me eating cucumbers in the bathroom?' Vrishabha fell at the king's feet. 'Forgive me, Oh king!' he said with great show of fear. 'I did not get a wink of sleep last night. My head is reeling. I do not know what I muttered. Please don't give it a moment's thought.'

At this the King began to wonder whether he had not been unjust to the poor merchant. He reflected: 'This imbecile has been talking utter nonsense about me. What he said about Vajradanta must be equally nonsensical. I should not have shown disfavour to the poor man. How could he have caressed the queen? He is a respectable man and can never be guilty of such misconduct. Moreover, since his downfall the city's business has suffered.' And so he summoned Vajradanta, loaded him with presents, and restored him to favour.

* * *

Having related the story of Vajradanta, Damanaka said, 'So you see that a king's servant cannot be trifled with. You will have to do as I say.' Sanjivaka replied, 'Of course, my dear friend. How can I ever go against your wishes?'

Damanaka led the bull to his master and, having introduced them to each other, retired. After exchanging civilities, Sanjivaka described how he had been stranded in the forest. Pingalaka listened with interest and said, 'You must now remain here without the slightest fear. My paws will protect you from all dangers. We shall enjoy many amusements together." And then, for the first time in many days, the lion went to the Yamuna's bank with a light heart. He drank his fill and bathed in the cool water. Then he roamed about in the forest, carefree as in former days. As time passed, the lion and the bull became intimate friends. A lively affection sprang up between them. Sanjivaka, who had studied many authoritative works on the subject of conduct and statesmanship, began to give lessons to his new comrade. The lion's wits were sharpened and he gratefully imbibed the education offered to him. Gradually he was weaned away from forest ways, became urbane, and acquired much refinement.

Indeed, Sanjivaka and Pingalaka spent so much time in each other's company that other animals were kept at a distance. With the lion's prowess lulled into inaction through the joys of friendship, very little hunting was done. Soon there was acute shortage of food. As for Damanaka, he was completely forgotten. No longer did he have right of entry into the king's inner circle. Pinched with hunger, he bemoaned his lot in the company of his friend Karataka. 'Alas, my friend,' he said, 'you have been proved right. Meddling has done us no good. Now our king takes so much delight in Sanjivaka's company that he does not give a thought to his own followers.'

Karataka said, 'Yes, we are in a spot all right. In introducing this grass-eater to the king you have been playing with fire. Now what are you going to do?'

'I must devise some method of separating the two friends. It is my duty, as a loyal servant, to save the king from his excessive fondness for the bull.'

'That is easier said than done. Have you the power to detach the king from this outsider?'

'Power is not everything. Sometimes shrewdness is enough, however difficult the goal may be. Let us remember how the crow killed the dreadful snake.'

Karataka said that he had not heard the story of the crow and the snake; so Damanaka narrated it.

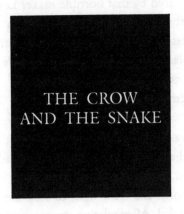

THE CROW
AND THE SNAKE

Once a crow and his wife made their nest on one of the lower branches of a huge banyan tree. By and by they became deeply attached to their home, and made it cosy and comfortable in every way. But their happiness did not last very long. A black snake took up his residence among the roots of the tree. He started crawling through the hollow trunk and eating their chicks as quickly as they were born.

When the crow and his wife had lost many of their young ones, the idea of leaving their nest was discussed between them. The crow-hen said to her husband, 'My dear, how long will you allow my children to be devoured by that horrible snake? Let us make our home elsewhere'. But the crow fell into depression at the thought of abandoning his nest. 'We have lived here a long time,' he said. 'How can we leave this place? After all it is our home. We should rather think of destroying our enemy.'

'But the enemy is cunning and powerful. How can you hurt him?'

'I may not have the power to kill him, but I have wise friends who have mastered all the works on diplomacy and warfare. They will show me a way out.'

With these words the crow went to seek the guidance of one of his dear friends, a jackal. After relating the cause of his sorrow the crow said, 'My friend, you must come to our rescue. My wife and myself are dying of grief at the thought of our dear little ones, so cruelly swallowed up by the black snake.'

'Do not worry,' said the jackal. 'There is an easy way out of your trouble. You must somehow get hold of a gold chain or necklace belonging to some king or wealthy nobleman. Then you should deposit the chain in the snake's home. The rest will be easy.'

Acting upon the jackal's advice the crow and his wife began to fly far and wide looking for a rich man's establishment or a royal camp. By and by they came to a pool where the women of the king's court were disporting themselves. They had taken off their jewels and laid them on the bank. Seizing her opportunity the crow-hen pounced upon one of the gold chains and picked it up with her beak. Then the crow and his wife hurried back homeward, pursued by the king's servants and soldiers. The crow-hen dropped the chain in the snakepit and watched.

The king's men, searching the tree with great thoroughness, discovered the hole. They explored the hole with their sticks until the snake came out with a swollen hood. The soldiers killed the snake with their clubs, recovered the chain, and returned to the camp.

And after that the crow and his wife lived peacefully in the home that they loved so much.

* * *

Damanaka continued, 'You can thus see, my friend, that force alone does not always decide. The story of the crow and the snake shows us what a clever device can achieve. But even more revealing is the story of the rabbit and the lion. It happened like this.'

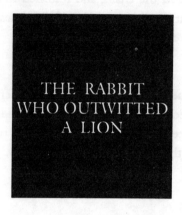

THE RABBIT WHO OUTWITTED A LION

There was once a lion named Bhasuraka. He was proud of his strength and killed the animals of the forest without mercy. So one day all the animals met in a conference and decided to approach the lion with a proposal. 'Oh, king,' they said, 'please do not kill us indiscriminately. Think of the other world. It is sinful to take life in excess of your needs. We propose that you remain at home and one animal be sent to you every day to satisfy your hunger. In this way your sustenance will continue and our families, too, will not be rooted out. A cow must not be milked every hour, but only in the morning. Remember that the loss of his subjects is also the king's loss. Have mercy, then, and accept our suggestion.'

The lion said, 'Gentlemen, your words are quite convincing. I accept the arrangement. But remember, if an animal does not come to me every day I shall destroy you all at a single stroke.' And so the animals began to roam the woods without fear, choosing one among them to serve as the King's meal every day. The different species sent their members by turns, selecting an individual who had become old, or indifferent to life through religious feelings.

One day it was the turn of the rabbits. The rabbit selected happened to be a plucky and clever fellow. Instead of going to his death meekly he made up his mind to try his wits and lead the lion to destruction. So he lingered on the way and deliberately arrived in the lion's presence several hours after the appointed time. The King was in a rage, vowing to exterminate all the animals the first thing next morning.

The rabbit approached at a leisurely pace, bowed low, and stood before the lion. Bhasuraka thundered, 'So, you are supposed to be my dinner! Measly thing, you are no more than a single morsel to me. And you dare to keep me waiting for hours! Is that how the animals keep their agreement? I shall kill every single one of them.'

The rabbit said with great show of respect, 'Master, the fault is not mine, nor are the other animals to blame. Something unexpected happened.'

'What happened? Tell me quickly, while you are still outside my jaws.'

'Master, as you see I am too small to satisfy your appetite. That is why five other rabbits were sent along with me. We were all coming here at the appointed time, but a lion emerged from a big hole under the ground and stopped us. 'Where are you going?' he asked. On our replying he said, 'Pray to your family deity. I want to eat you.' We replied, 'You have no right to eat us. We are the dinner of Bhasuraka, our mighty king.' At this he jeered at us and said, 'This forest belongs to me. Bhasuraka is a thief. Bring him here at once and I shall show you who is the master.' And so he detained my comrades, sending me to you with his challenge. That is why, Oh King, I could not come in time.'

'Who is this rascal?' said Bhasuraka. 'Lead me to him at once. I shall have no peace of mind until I drive him away.'

The rabbit said, 'Quite so. A true warrior brooks no insult. But you must be cautious. This fellow lives in a fortress. And a single fortress is equal in might to a thousand elephants.'

'I don't care where he hides. I shall kill him all the same. An enemy must be destroyed at once. He must never be permitted to grow.'

'Very well. But it was my duty to warn you of your enemy's strength. You must not underestimate him.'

'What business is it of yours, you imp? Show me this fortress.'

Thereupon the rabbit led Bhasuraka to a deep well and said, 'Master, your very approach has terrified the thief. He has crawled into his hole. You can see him if you peep into it.'

The lion peeped into the well and saw his own reflection in the water. Fool that he was, he mistook the reflection for a real lion and roared loudly. The sound reissued from the well with redoubled loudness. At this Bhasuraka was mad with anger, hurled himself upon his imaginary rival, and met his death. The rabbit carried the happy news to the animals, who thereafter lived contentedly in the forest.

* * *

Karataka, having listened to the story of the rabbit's cleverness, said, 'Don't you think, my friend, that this is an exceptional case? I still hold that a person of feeble powers should not try to be tricky with great people.'

Damanaka retorted, 'Feeble or strong, one must take determined action when the occasion demands it. The Gods are on the side of those who are vigorous in their efforts.'

And so, determined to retrieve his position, Damanaka again went to meet Pingalaka. The King welcomed him and asked him what he wanted. Damanaka answered, 'Master, I bring tidings that are important, though unpleasant. No devoted attendant likes to carry bad news, and yet loyalty demands that the truth must be told, so that immediate action may be taken.'

'Come, come, my good fellow,' said Pingalaka. 'What is all this about?'

'Oh King, prepare yourself for a shock. This fellow, Sanjivaka, has gained your confidence for treacherous ends. He has been examining your strength and weakness, your advisers and material resources. His plan is to kill you and seize royal power for himself. And I have reason to believe that he is intending to carry out his design very soon. That is why I have hastened here to warn you.'

This report came to Pingalaka like a bolt from the blue. For a while he was sunk in a stupor and did not say a word. Damanaka, pretending to be in great distress, said, 'Alas, how difficult and depressing is a counsellor's task. With what sadness he must discharge his duty! Your Majesty, do you not see that Sanjivaka already manages state affairs without any restraint? He is only waiting for the final step.'

'But why should he change so suddenly? Moreover, even if he has changed, I cannot consider him to be my enemy. Once dear is always dear, even if there are signs of fickleness. Our bodies may become decrepit, but we cling to them all the same. And similarly our heart clings to a loved one, even if his actions are improper.'

'Yes, it does. That is why it is so difficult to get on in the world. But a wise person, and especially a wise king, must abandon a traitor, dear though he be. Let us remember the song that the women sing.

'What is the good of golden earrings, if they lacerate your ears?' Towards a person such as Sanjivaka, pity is out of place. I must speak out, though truth is seldom flattering. A king should never leave tried servants and hearken to strangers.'

By this time Pingalaka's confidence in his friend had already become shaky. 'When he appeared as a suppliant,' he said, 'I gave him safe-conduct. How can he prove ungrateful?' But Damanaka retorted, 'A rogue does not ask a reason before he shows hostility. You may feed a dog on dainties, but you cannot straighten his tail. It is no use offering perfume to a corpse. It is a waste of energy to plant lotuses in dry earth. Never trust an ungrateful fellow, otherwise you will repent, like the Brahmin who rescued the goldsmith.'

Pingalaka said he had never heard the story. So Damanaka narrated it.

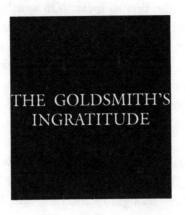

THE GOLDSMITH'S INGRATITUDE

There was once a Brahmin named Tyaga. He was poor and his wife always scolded him. 'Get up, you lazy Brahmin', she would say, 'Be up and doing, you idler. Don't you see that the children are starving? Go and get some food.'

At last, tired of hearing these taunts, the Brahmin left his home and set out on a long journey. After a few days he entered a dense forest. Pached with thirst, he searched for water and eventually came upon a well. When he looked in, he discovered that a tiger, a monkey, a snake and a man had fallen into the well. All of them saw the Brahmin and the hope of rescue dawned in their hearts.

The tiger was the first to speak. 'Oh worthy Brahmin,' he said 'there is great merit in saving life. Please pull me out so that I may return and join my family.'

'Indeed!' said the Brahmin, 'the very mention of a tiger makes me shiver. And you want me to pull you out?'

'I give my word of honour,' the tiger said, 'that no harm will come to you. Please have mercy and save me. You will see that I shall always be grateful.'

And so the Brahmin pulled out the tiger. After a while he rescued the monkey also. Then the snake, too, cried for help. The Brahmin shuddered at the very thought of touching him, but when the snake repeatedly promised that he would not bite, the Brahmin pulled him out. All the three animals expressed their thankfulness and invited the Brahmin to their respective homes.

The tiger said, 'My cave is in a wooded ravine on the slope of that mountain. You must call on me so that I might repay the debt of your kindness to some extent.'

The monkey said, 'By the side of the cave that my friend has mentioned there is a waterfall. My home is just near the waterfall. Do come whenever you feel like it.'

The snake was very brief. He simply said, 'Remember me in the hour of need.'

Meanwhile the man, who was still at the bottom of the well, was shouting for help. All the three animals warned the Brahmin against rescuing him. 'The man is a villain,' they said. 'Never trust him.' But he cried so piteously that the Brahmin was moved. He thought: 'After all he is a man like me. How can I leave him in the well, when I have just rescued these animals?' And so he pulled out the man too.

'I am a goldsmith,' said the man. 'If you have any gold to be worked into shape bring it to me.' With these words he started for home. And the animals, too, went their respective ways.

The Brahmin continued his wanderings for a long time. When at last he started for home he remembered the monkey's invitation. He visited the monkey's home and was received with great affection. The Brahmin enjoyed the delicious fruits offered to him. Then, satisfied that the monkey had shown his gratitude, he visited the tiger. There, too, he was treated with utmost cordiality. And when the Brahmin said farewell to him, the tiger gave him many gold ornaments. 'These belong to a prince whom I once killed in the forest,' he said. 'Take them, my friend, as a humble token of gratitude.'

The Brahmin thought that by selling the jewels he would get enough money to live comfortably with his family. And then he suddenly thought of the goldsmith whom he had saved from the well. He said to himself: 'Surely I can get these gold ornaments sold at a proper price through the help of my friend. After all I *did* save his life.' So he visited the goldsmith and told him what he wanted.

The goldsmith offered him a seat and placed food and water near him. Then he said, 'Please remain here while I show your gold to an expert.' And, slipping out of the house, he went straight to the king's palace. There he informed the officers that a Brahmin with stolen property was in his house. The officers lost no time in arresting the Brahmin. He was put in fetters and the king ordered him to be executed the next morning. The man had abandoned all hope when he suddenly remembered the snake's words: 'Think of me in an emergency.' So he called upon the snake to help him.

The snake immediately appeared and, when he was apprised of the situation, said, 'I see a way out of this. I shall bite the king's favourite queen. All the conjurers and physicians will fail to cure her. As soon as you touch her I shall withdraw the poison. The king will not only release you but lavish favours upon you.'

The plan was carried out. The snake bit the queen and there was great commotion in the palace. All the antidotes were tried, druggists and snake-charmers were summoned. When everyone failed, the Brahmin offered to cure her. He was led to the queen's chamber and at the mere touch of his hand the poison was neutralized.

The Brahmin received great honour and wealth. He revealed to the king how the goldsmith had betrayed him, while the animals whom he had rescued had proved their gratitude. The king arrested the goldsmith and appointed the Brahmin to a high office.

* * *

'That is why,' Damanaka said, 'I am warning you about this Sanjivaka. The fact that you have been kind to him is no guarantee of his gratitude. Moreover, since your association with the bull you have neglected all the three values of kingship—virtue, wealth and love. The administration has slowed down, conquests have stopped and loyal friends have been neglected.'

Pingalaka was considerably shaken by Damanaka's arguments. 'Well, what should I do?' he asked. 'Shall I warn him?'

'Warn him? That would be the most disastrous policy. Does a wise person ever warn an enemy? Not by a word, nor by a gesture must you arouse his suspicions.'

'But, after all, he is a mere grass-eater. How can he do me any harm?'

'Yes, he is a grass-eater. But he may carry out his plan through others who are not. Whichever way you look at it, the situation is dangerous. My lord, let me repeat that a king must not neglect his trusted servants. Whoever leaves his friends and cherishes strangers suffers. Think of what happened to the blue jackal.'

But Pingalaka had never heard of the blue jackal. So Damanaka related the following story.

THE BLUE
JACKAL

Once a jackal named
Chandarava lived near the suburbs of a city. One day hunger goaded
him inside the city where he roamed the streets, looking for food. The
city dogs barked at him and snapped at his limbs with their sharp teeth,
until the poor jackal was terrified. He fled blindly, trying to escape
from the dogs, and strayed into a dyer's house. There he fell into an
indigo tub and lay concealed for many hours.

At dawn he managed to crawl out of the tub and somehow
reached the forest, his body dyed a deep blue. All the animals of the
forest gaped at him in amazement. They thought that an exotic creature

had mysteriously appeared, and, scared for their lives, kept at a distance.

Taking advantage of their dismay, Chandarava called to them, 'Now, now, you foolish creatures! Don't be afraid. Indra has taken mercy on you. Since you had no monarch Indra has anointed me as your king. My name is Chandarava. You may live peacefully under my protection.'

At this all the animals of the forest—lions, tigers, monkeys, leopards, elephants, rabbits and the rest—bowed before him and swore loyalty. 'Oh, master;' they said, 'tell us our duties, and we shall carry them out.' So Chandarava appointed a lion as his chief minister, a tiger as his personal valet and a leopard as the custodian of his betel-box. An elephant was made the doorkeeper and a monkey was placed in charge of the royal umbrella. But when jackals came near him he insulted them and drove them away, although they were his own kith and kin.

In this way Chandarava lived in kingly glory. Lions and tigers killed animals for him and he ate the most delicious morsels. And then he distributed the remainder of the food in a grand, royal manner.

One day, while he was sitting in his court, he heard the noise made by a pack of jackals nearby. At this his body quivered with pleasure and tears of joy filled his eyes. He jumped up and gave vent to a piercing howl. For a moment the animals surrounding him were stunned. But soon they understood the situation and felt ashamed at the discovery that they had been imposed upon by a mere jackal. They pounced on him. Chandarava tried to escape but a tiger pursued him and tore him to bits.

* * *

'That is why,' Damanaka continued, 'I say that one's own friends should never be abandoned. Whoever does so comes to grief.'

Pingalaka said, 'You are right. But I am still not convinced that

Sanjivaka wants to attack me. Can you describe some of the gestures by which I may guess his aggressive designs?'

'Certainly,' said Damanaka. 'If he comes in your presence with his limbs relaxed, with horns bent to one side, and if he approaches you timidly, you should conclude that he harbours treachery in his mind.'

'Very well, I shall watch out for these symptoms,' said Pingalaka. Damanaka took his leave. After a while he went back to the bull, and put up a show of depression. Sanjivaka asked him, 'What is the matter, my friend? You seem to be in low spirits.' Damanaka said, 'Alas, he who waits upon a king must endure a never-ending succession of worries. His life is not his own. He must pass sleepless nights.'

Sanjivaka was baffled. 'You are hiding something from me,' he said. 'You must tell me what is bothering you.'

'I suppose I must, however unpleasant the task might be. It is on your account that I am in misery. The master has turned against you. He is determined to kill you and feed all his followers on your body. Ever since I came to know this, I am utterly dejected.'

At this Sanjivaka began to shake with fear. 'What evil fate is mine!' he exclaimed. 'I served the king most loyally and showed nothing but friendship towards him. If a friend is angry for a cause one can remove it. But how can anyone pacify causeless wrath. Alas, what wrong have I done to your master?'

'Don't be a simpleton. Kings often love to inflict injuries without reason. Serpents defile sandal trees and crocodiles lurk in lotus pools. Likewise, malice often dwells in royal hearts. You must never place your trust in a king. He may be all honey at first, but he turns into poison when it suits him, or when he is misguided by unscrupulous people. Remember what sad fate overtook Krathanaka, the camel, when he trusted the lion.'

Sanjivaka said, 'I would like to hear the story of this camel.' And so Damanaka told him this story.

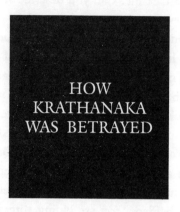

HOW
KRATHANAKA
WAS BETRAYED

Once a rich merchant set out on a long journey with valuable brocades and other goods loaded on a pack of camels. After traversing a long distance one of the camels, whose name was Krathanaka, was overcome with fatigue. As the merchant was not in a position to linger at that place he left the camel behind and proceeded. In course of time Krathanaka recovered his strength and made his way to a forest nearby.

In this forest there lived a lion named Madotkata. He had for his intimate companions a leopard, a crow and a jackal. They saw the camel from a distance and were surprised by his strange shape. The lion approached him and asked, 'My dear fellow, who are you and where have you come from?' Krathanaka described in detail how he was taken ill and stranded, at which the lion felt pity and guaranteed his personal security. So the camel joined their company and was treated as a friend.

One day the lion received a thrust from an elephant's tusk and was severely wounded. He had to keep to his cave. A week passed and he was still unable to hunt. His companions began to feel the pangs of hunger. The lion felt sad but was helpless. 'Round up some animal,' he said, 'and bring him near me. Even in my present condition I will manage to kill him.'

The companions roamed far and wide but were unable to round up any animal that could have served as food. So the crow and the jackal met separately and hatched a plot. 'My friend,' said the jackal, 'why must we wander in the woods in search of food? Here is this camel. He trusts our king, and he is big enough to last us for quite some time.'

'An excellent idea,' said the crow. 'But do you think the Master will agree to kill him? He has guaranteed the camel's security.'

'No harm trying. I will try to persuade the Master.' With these words the jackal went to the lion's cave and said, 'Master, we searched the entire forest but were unable to round up a suitable animal. We are now too tired to move a muscle. Moreover, we are pained to see you fasting. There is only one thing to do. We have got to kill Krathanaka.'

Madotkata was horrified by the proposal. 'Shame on you,' he said. 'Never dare to repeat the suggestion or I will strike you dead. I promised his personal security. How can I kill him?'

The jackal, having failed to persuade the lion, now changed his tactics. 'I agree with you, Master,' he said, 'It would be sinful to kill him without provocation. But it would be quite another matter if he were to offer his life to you out of devotion and gratitude. No blame would attach to you in that case. However, if this is not possible you must kill us one by one. What is the worth of our miserable lives if they cannot be spent in your service? Moreover, if you were to die of hunger we shall, in any case, plunge into the funeral pyre out of grief. Since we have to die either way, why not kill us and sustain your strength?'

These words made a deep impression on Madotkata. The idea of killing his own companions was abhorrent to him. He reluctantly agreed to kill the camel provided the latter voluntarily offered himself.

The jackal rejoined his friends and said, 'Gentlemen, the Master's condition is critical. Hunger has laid him low. He is sinking. If the king goes, what will happen to this forest? Let us go and offer him our own bodies. In this way we shall pay our debt of gratitude to him and also earn merit for the life to come.'

So they all went and sat down with tearful eyes by the side of Madotkata. The crow was the first to speak. 'Oh, beloved Master,' he cried, 'please eat me and support your life at least for half a day. Please give me this chance of acquiring heavenly bliss.'

The jackal cut him short and said, 'Friend crow, this is indeed noble of you. But your body is so small that the Master cannot satisfy his hunger by eating you. You have shown your loyalty. Now make way and let me do my duty.' With these words the jackal bowed low and addressed the lion with half-shut eyes. 'Master, please utilize my body and lengthen your life. The life of a servant is eternally forfeit to his Lord in lieu of the pay he receives. By taking away this life the Master commits no sin. On the contrary he bestows upon the servant the merit of saintliness.'

Not to be outdone, the leopard said, 'Excellent, my friend, excellent. But I am afraid even your body is rather too small. Besides, it would not be proper for the Master to eat you. If you will forgive my saying so, your family hardly constitutes food fit for a king. You have done your bit; now let me win the Master's grace.' And so the leopard bowed low before Madotkata and, with great show of devotion, begged to be eaten.

When he heard all these touching offers, Krathanaka thought: 'What elegant phrases these fellows have been using! And yet the Master has not touched any of them. I think I should also make a speech worthy of the occasion. These three will, I know, contradict me.' And so he said, 'Friend leopard, how can the Master eat you? You are his kinsman. Make way for me.'

And then, turning to the lion, he said, 'Master, none of these are worthy to be eaten. Please prolong your life by consuming my body so that I may win merit everlasting.'

As soon as he had uttered these words the lion gave the signal. The leopard and the jackal tore up poor Krathanaka's body, and the crow pecked out his eyes. And all of them, famished as they were, devoured him.

* * *

Having heard this story Sanjivaka was convinced that, in spite of the safe conduct promised by him, Pingalaka would not hesitate to kill him. So he asked Damanaka, 'My friend, give me some tips. How can I guess the King's intentions?'

Damanaka answered, 'Why, that is easy. As you know, he usually sits on a slab of stone with his limbs relaxed. If you find that now his tail is drawn in, paws gathered together, and ears pricked up, and if you detect a watchful look in his eyes while you are still far off, you may be sure that he is bent upon treachery.'

When Damanaka was gone, Sanjivaka took stock of the situation. 'What am I to do?' he thought. 'I might go away elsewhere, but then some other creature will kill me. After all, this is a jungle. Alas, when the Master is furious·one cannot feel safe even in flight. The only course open to me is to approach the lion. When he sees me as a suppliant he might spare my life.'

And having come to this conclusion he slowly started, troubled in spirit and shaking with fear. When he was still far off he saw Pingalaka in the posture described by Damanaka. He was convinced that the lion had decided to kill him. So he instinctively bent his horns and approached timidly.

Pingalaka, in his turn, saw the bull in the attitude predicted by Damanaka. So he made a sudden spring at his former friend. Sanjivaka, though his body was torn by sharp claws, attacked the lion's belly with his horns, and managed to break away from him. Both of them stood in fighting postures, ready to fall upon each other.

Damanaka and Karataka were watching the fight from a distance. They had been friends for a long time. But now Karataka was revolted by the tragic results of his friend's conspiracy. 'You fool,' he said. 'What have you done! In setting these two at enmity you have done a wicked deed. You have brought trouble and confusion to the entire forest. You claim to be a counsellor. Don't you know that a counsellor's duty is to try conciliation first and last? What calamitous advice have you given our Master! You could not see the two of them happy, and so you have broken up their friendship. Even I can trust you no longer. Who can count on a friend like you? It is much better to associate with a farsighted enemy than with a stupid friend. After all, the robber died for his own victims.'

'What robber are you talking about?' asked Damanaka; and Karataka told him the following story.

THE
THOUGHTFUL
ENEMY

There was once a prince who had two close companions—a merchant's son and a scholar's son. The three of them passed their time in various diversions and entertainments, both literary and otherwise. The prince had no interest left in archery, hunting, the science of warfare and other royal occupations. At last one day his father rebuked him roundly for his indifference to kingly pursuits.

The prince told his friends how severely the king had upbraided him. They rejoined that their fathers, too, had similar ideas and had often pulled them up for their indifference towards commerce and scholarship respectively. The prince said, 'My friends, we are all in the same boat. We share a common grief. We have all been insulted by our fathers. We cannot remain here any longer. Let us go somewhere else.'

Then they fell to discussing where it would be advisable to go. The merchant's son said, 'No desire can be fulfilled without money. Let us go to the Mountain of Prosperity. There, if luck is with us, we shall find precious gems. And with this wealth we can proceed to enjoy all that we crave for.'

And so they journeyed to the Mountain of Prosperity. Guided by a friendly providence each of them found a priceless gem. But when they began their return journey, a doubt arose in their minds. Knowing that they would have to pass through deep forests, they were frightened at the prospect of being attacked by bandits. Pondering over their predicament, they at last decided to swallow the gems and carry them in their stomachs. In this way, they felt, even the most thorough search of their persons would not reveal their wealth.

During their next meal each inserted his gem in a mouthful of food and swallowed it. While they were doing so, a man resting on the slope of the mountain watched them. He reflected: 'What luck! I have been tramping this mountain side for days and have found nothing, while these fellows have discovered magnificent gems. I shall become their travelling companion and, when they are sunk in sleep, I shall despatch them. Then I can cut open their stomachs and secure the gems.'

With this evil thought in his mind the man descended from the mountain, approached them, and said, 'Gentlemen, I lack the courage to travel through the forest all by myself. Will you be so good as to admit me in your group? I shall be most grateful to you, and you may rest assured that I shall not be a burden.' The three friends, being friendly and unsuspecting by nature, agreed, and all of them continued the journey together. While passing through the forest they reached a village inhabited by robbers. Their chief kept a number of caged birds in his hut. He understood the meaning of all their songs and thus often acquired strange information. Now one of these birds began to sing as soon as he saw the four travellers. The chief of the robbers heard the song with great delight. He summoned his followers and said, 'Just listen to the bird's song. He says there are precious gems in the possession of those travellers. Catch them and bring them here.'

The robbers, obeying their orders, rounded up the travellers and led them to the chief's hut. The chief thoroughly searched the travellers with his own hands but found nothing. So he set them free. But as soon as they had been freed the bird sang the same song again. This. happened a number of times, until the chief got angry and said, 'I have tested this bird again and again. He never tells lies. Where are the gems? Out with them!' The travellers protested saying, 'If we had any gems would you not have discovered them? You have carried out a most careful search.' But the chief retorted, 'I don't know about that. The bird says over and over again that the gems are in your possession. They must be inside your stomachs. It is now evening. I spare you for the night. Tomorrow morning I shall cut you open.' And with these words he flung them in a dark cell.

Now the thief who had joined the three companions with evil intentions reflected: 'Alas, in the morning I must die. Along with the others I shall also be killed. It is best, then, that I should offer my own body first. In this way I may be able to save the men whom I had wickedly planned to kill. When my stomach is cut open and the robber-chief finds nothing precious in it, he will reconsider the idea of killing the others. Heartless though he is, he will shrink from needless murder. Thus by saving their lives and wealth I shall be doing a generous deed and shall gain merit. That will be a wise man's death.'

At dawn the chief of the robbers dragged the travellers out of the cell and prepared to slash their bellies. The thief among them clasped his hands in prayer and said, 'At least grant me this favour. Cut my belly first so that I may not have to witness the butchering of my brothers.' The chief agreed, and with one stroke of his sword killed him. But when he did not find any gems in the dead man's belly he repented his action. 'What a stupid thing have I done!' he said. 'Guided by a mere bird I have killed a man from whom I could gain nothing. The others, too, have probably been telling me the truth. There may be no gems in their stomachs, after all.'

And so he released the travellers who, crossing the forest unharmed, reached the city with their wealth intact.

* * *

'That is why,' Karataka continued, 'I feel that it is better to have a wise enemy than a stupid friend. You, whom our Master trusted, have been the cause of his disaster. You have done wrong, and a person like you must be shunned.'

Karataka's denunciation was lost upon his friend. Lessons in morality held no appeal for him. So he quietly edged away. Meanwhile Pingalaka and Sanjivaka had renewed their battle. Very soon the bull's resistance was over, and Pingalaka killed him. When he saw his beloved friend lying dead, the lion's anger melted away. He was overwhelmed by grief and repentance. 'Alas, what have I done!' he bewailed. 'Sanjivaka was my dearest friend, and I have killed him with my own hands. How could I do such a monstrous thing?' And then, wiping his tears with his blood-smeared paw, Pingalaka sobbed for a long time.

Karataka approached him and drove home the lesson of the great calamity. 'All this has happened, Sir,' he said, 'because you trusted a single adviser, and an unscrupulous one at that. A king is always surrounded by petty individuals who are waiting to lead their Master astray. When they succeed, that is the end of royal glory. A monarch should always consult his counsellors separately and then arrive at his own decision. Sometimes things appear in a false light. A firefly is mistaken for a spark of fire and the sky looks flat. Likewise an argument may look very convincing, but the king must examine it closely to see if it is really sound. He must always consider the ultimate issue and take into account the complexities of every situation. Above all he must be his own master.'

In this way Karataka gave befitting advice to the lion. The damage, however, had already been done. A tender friendship had been broken up, the kingdom had suffered through suspense and strife, and an innocent and valuable companion had been killed. And all this because Pingalaka, the King of the Forest, had allowed himself to be led away by a greedy and malicious jackal.

BOOK TWO

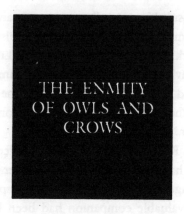

THE ENMITY
OF OWLS AND
CROWS

On the outskirts of a prosperous city in the southern country there was once a mighty banyan tree, with countless branches spread over a vast area. In this tree there lived a tribe of crows ruled by a wise king named Meghavarna. The king was just and his subjects were loyal. All of them lived together happily and peacefully among the branches of that huge tree.

They had, however, one great source of anxiety. As the result of an ancient grudge, a king of owls, Arimardana by name, had taken to killing Meghavarna's subjects. Whenever, in the course of his wanderings, Arimardana came across a crow, he killed him on the spot and passed on merrily.

When this continued for some time Meghavarna summoned all his advisers and said, 'Gentlemen, the situation is serious. Our enemy is proud and powerful. He always comes after dark and causes panic in our ranks. We cannot counterattack because by night we are helpless and in the day the enemy hides himself in his fortress. What shall we do? Let us meet in a secret session and chalk out a course of action. Shall we make peace, or go to war? Shall we change our base or entrench ourselves? Shall we seek allies or take recourse to deception? Speak up, gentlemen.'

The king had five ancestral counsellors. Their names were Ujjivi, Sanjivi, Anujivi, Prajivi and Sthirajivi. Meghavarna first turned to Ujjivi and asked his opinion.

Ujjivi replied, 'Your Majesty, I am in favour of peace. One should not make war against a powerful enemy. Besides, war brings disaster to every one. We must never stir a quarrel; we should rather endure pain. Under the enemy's pressure we should bend like a reed rather than strike back like a serpent. The cloud does not make war against the wind, though the wind is bent upon scattering it.'

The king next asked the opinion of Sanjivi. He said, 'Sir, I disagree. The enemy is greedy, merciless and without principles. With such people conciliation is impossible. We should rather fight and try our fortunes in the battlefield. He has humiliated us. If we propose peace, he will fall upon us with redoubled vigour. Conciliation only feeds an enemy's violence, like drops of water sprinkled on boiling butter. My friend Ujjivi refers to the enemy's power and strength. But this argument is not decisive. The small can often kill the great through energy and skill. The lion gets the better of the elephant. We may be small, but that is no reason why we may not defeat the owls. No, Sir. Peace is ruled out. I am for war.'

It was Anujivi's turn to give his opinion. He put on a cautious expression and slowly said, 'The enemy is vicious and powerful. Peace and war are both fraught with dangers. In my opinion the only way is to change our headquarters. Thereby we can retreat for the time being, in order to invade at the right moment. The matter has been discussed by the classical writers with due regard to cause and effect. Often in the past mighty kings have abandoned their realms in order to stage a victorious counterattack. Even rams draw back before attacking vigourously. And the lion's spring is most deadly when he crouches before he strikes. We must not make this a question of pride. We have to do what the occasion demands. The present moment is no time for either peace or war.'

At this Prajivi said, 'Oh King, I am afraid I cannot approve of any of these suggestions. Change of base will do no good. A crocodile at home can defeat even an elephant, but on alien territory even a dog can harass it. We should neither make overtures of peace nor launch an offensive, nor change our headquarters. We must firmly entrench ourselves here and wait till the enemy's strength is exhausted. If an army stands firm, well equipped with all the materials, the besiegers feel helpless. Let us unite and stick confidently to our ancestral home.'

Meghavarna then turned to Chiranjivi and asked, 'My friend, what have you to say?' Chiranjivi said. 'In my opinion what we need is the friendship of strong allies. Without friends no struggle can be successfully waged. Even the fire needs the support of the wind. It is not necessary to leave our home, but it *is* necessary that we obtain assistance from outside. The ally we seek need not be powerful. Even two weak friends can score over a single powerful enemy.'

Having heard these opinions Meghavarna turned towards a venerable old crow named Sthirajivi. Farsighted and wise, resourceful and thoroughly conversant with all the textbooks of political science, Sthirajivi was the patriarch among Meghavarna's advisers. The king looked upon him as a father and, at a moment of crisis, his judgment was considered final. Now Meghavarna, in sore need of his help, said, 'Sir, I have questioned others in your presence with a definite purpose. I desired that you might listen to all their suggestions and then guide me along the course you deem best.'

Sthirajivi said, 'My son, I have carefully heard their opinions. They have drawn upon standard works on diplomacy and military science. Each course is proper in its own place. But just now what we need is duplicity. We must not pin our faith either in peace or in war, nor in other measures that have been suggested. We have to gain the enemy's trust and then destroy him. And this we can do by discovering a vulnerable point.'

'But,' Meghavarna protested, 'I do not know their castle. How shall I discover their weak point?'

Sthirajivi replied, 'Have patience, my son. Through spies the necessary information will be obtained. And another thing—you must never forget the background of the struggle between the owls and ourselves. You must keep the historical sequence in mind.'

Meghavarna requested Sthirajivi to describe the origin of the conflict between the two tribes of birds. And the venerable counsellor narrated the following chronicle.

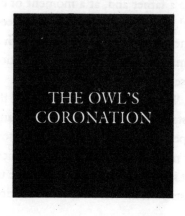

THE OWL'S CORONATION

Once upon a time all the birds gathered in a forest. There were cranes and nightingales, doves and partridges, skylarks and cuckoos, peacocks and woodpeckers and many others.

The problem before them was stated by one of the birds in this way: 'Gentlemen, we must choose a king. It is true that Garuda is supposed to be our monarch. But all his time is taken up in the service of Vishnu. He hardly ever bothers about us. What is the good of an absentee king? When we are in distress he is nowhere near at hand. If we are caught in traps, he cannot rescue us. A king like him is like a leaky ship. Let us, then, select some one who will be a king in fact, not just a king in name.'

Now, while this proposal was being made, all the birds had turned their attention to the owl. He looked so solemn, so earnest and venerable, that they said, 'Well, why delay matters? Let the owl be our king. And let us have the coronation as early as possible.'

And so preparations for the anointing ceremony were commenced right away. Birds were despatched to various holy streams in order to fetch pure water. A bouquet was made out of the traditionally prescribed leaves and flowers, including the yellow lotus. A map of the seven continents, mountains, and oceans was drawn up, symbolising the future king's glorious conquests. A tiger-skin was spread upon the throne. Golden jars were filled with rice and decorated with twigs and blossoms. Brahmins were hired to recite the Vedas. Poets chanted verses from the epics. Maidens sang festive ditties. Holiday-drums rumbled. And the owl was led in a procession towards the spot where the ritual was to take place.

Just when he had taken his seat, a crow came there, heaven knows why and where from. He cawed raucously, as crows always do when they want to attract attention.

Looking around, he was baffled by the grand preparations. 'What's all the fuss about?' he thought. 'Must be some great festival.' Meanwhile the birds had seen him. They had all heard that crows were exceedingly shrewd. And so they thought that his advice should be taken about the choice they had just made. One of them approached him and said, 'Friend crow, as you know we birds have no king—at least not the kind of a king who might really rule over us. We have chosen this owl as a worthy candidate for the throne. What is your opinion?'

The crow burst into laughter. For some time he was unable to speak, so great was his amusement. At last he looked at them pityingly and said, 'Gentlemen, is this a joke or is it plain foolishness? I see among you such eminent people as peacocks, cranes, swans, and nightingales. And yet you choose this ugly fellow, blind in the day and stupid by day as well as night! Just look at his hooked nose, his squinting eyes, and the rest of him. Just now he is in a good temper, as he has every reason to be. And yet he looks repulsive. What would he look like if he were to get angry? Moreover, Garuda is there already. To have two kings is like asking for two suns in the sky. Garuda has prestige. His name carries weight. What impression would the mention of an owl make on anybody? No, no, gentlemen. A king must have some status. Surely you remember how the rabbit fulfilled an extremely difficult assignment merely by mentioning a great name.'

'How was that?' asked the birds, and the crow told them this story.

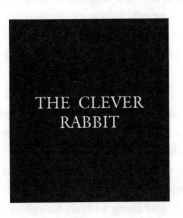

THE CLEVER RABBIT

There was once a great elephant-king named Chaturdanta. He ruled over a large band of elephants and spent his time in carrying out his royal duties faithfully. His subjects were devoted to him.

But who can contend against misfortune?

Once there was a failure of rain for twelve years in succession. All the tanks, ponds and lakes went dry. Every tree, shrub and creeper shrivelled up. At last the elephants said to their king, 'Sir, our little ones are tortured by thirst. Some of them are dead and others are gasping for breath. Pray devise some method of obtaining water.'

Moved by their plight, the king despatched reliable messenger-elephants in every direction to search for water.

Those who went east found a lake named Chandrasarovara. It was a beautiful spot indeed. The shores of the lake were adorned with trees of many kinds. The trees groaned under the weight of blossoms, while birds of beautiful plumage twittered and sang among their branches. The lake had crystal clear water, beautified with clusters of many-coloured lilies. Swans, ducks, herons and other aquatic creatures lived peacefully in that lake.

Enchanted by this sight, the scouts hastened back and reported to the king. Chaturdanta decided to migrate to the lake. He wound up his establishment, and along with all his subjects travelled by stages to the shores of Chandrasarovara. Now, as it happened, a large tribe of rabbits had made their home near the lake. Many of them were crushed to death under the feet of the elephants. Others were wounded and crippled. Many lost their young ones, their friends or their parents. And the elephants did not even notice the destruction they had caused.

Those rabbits who had luckily survived held a convention. 'What are we to do?' they said. 'These brutes will come every day and very soon our entire race will be wiped out.' Thereupon a rabbit named Vijaya heroically offered to try his wits against the elephants. 'Have no fear, my friends,' he said. 'I shall see to it that the elephants go away from here.'

The king of the rabbits said, 'This is a deed of valour that you have offered to do. I appoint you my envoy. Look after yourself. May providence smile upon your efforts.'

So Vijaya approached the king of the elephants. He was surrounded by many lordly elephants whose ears swayed like the branches of trees. The king looked like a mighty cloud to which flashes of lightning cling. His trumpeting was deep like the sound of a thunderbolt. His tusks were the colour of honey. Fragrant ichor-juice trickled from his temples, attracting a swarm of bees.

Vijaya thought: 'I must not go too near this stupendous fellow. An elephant can kill you by the mere touch. Let me find a safe place from where I can talk to him.'

He found a suitable spot on a pile of rocks. Perched there, he said to the elephant in a squeaky voice, 'How goes it with you, Oh Lord of the two-tusked species?' The elephant-king was surprised at being thus addressed. His narrow eyes peered this way and that. At last he said dubiously, 'And pray who may *you* be, Sir?'

'I am an envoy, of course', said the rabbit.

'An envoy? In whose service?'

'In the service of the Blessed Moon.'

'Well, in that case please state your business.'

The rabbit had not failed to notice that the elephant was already impressed. He carried through his advantage and said with an air of great importance, 'Sir, you must know that envoys enjoy special privileges. No injury must be done to them. Now hear my message. My Master asks of you:

How have you dared to do violence to others, grossly misjudging your own power? Are you looking for disaster? This lake is known by my sacred name. The whole world calls it the Lake of the Moon. And you have, near this very lake, killed and wounded rabbits who are under my protection. These rabbits are descended from the rabbit-king whom I cherish so dearly that I always clasp him to my bosom. Every living creature in the world knows about the rabbit in the moon. You alone seem to be ignorant. Now desist from such impertinence, otherwise I shall withdraw my light from you—the light by which you and your companions roam about in the forest so happily. Without my light you will be scorched by the heat and will soon perish, along with your subjects.'

The elephant-king heard this with awe and amazement. He was

silent for a while, and then said, 'Sir, you are right. I have indeed sinned against the Blessed Moon. Now please point out to me how I can go and ask his forgiveness.'

'Very well,' said the rabbit. 'But you must come alone. And see that you mind your manners.'

So when it was dark the rabbit escorted the elephant to the shore of the lake and pointed to the moon reflected in the water. The brilliant disc, surrounded by planets and stars, quivered on the lake's crystal-clear surface. With great deference the elephant said, 'I bow to the Blessed Moon and purify myself.' With these words he dipped his trunk in the water. As he did so the water was disturbed and the reflection of the moon danced this way and that.

Vijaya started back as if a great sacrilege had been committed. 'Stop, oh rash elephant,' he exclaimed. 'Do you want to anger the moon beyond all limits?'

The elephant said very humbly, 'My friend, in what way have I offended your master?'

'By touching this water, which is sacred, and belongs exclusively to the Moon and his attendants,' Vijaya said.

Chaturdanta touched the earth in homage, and in all humility begged the moon's forgiveness. Then, treading very gently, he went away, never to return. And from that moment onwards the rabbits were left in peace.

* * *

'That is why' the crow continued, 'I believe that a great name makes all the difference. This miserable owl whom you have selected has no status at all. If you make him your king, you will only be placing yourself in his power. Remember, you are blind at night while he can see well enough to do what he pleases.'

When the birds had heard the crow's remarks they felt ashamed of their haste in choosing the owl for the throne. So they slipped away to their homes, intending to reassemble at some other time to discuss the question. Meanwhile the owl, being blind in the day time, saw nothing of what was going on. He remained seated on the throne that had been set up. After a while he called out, 'You, there! Why is the ceremony delayed? Who takes my orders?'

At this his escort said, 'Sir, there is no one here. The crow has somehow broken up the ceremony. All the birds have flown away and only the crow remains. Arise, Your Majesty, I shall conduct you home.'

The owl's disappointment was as great as his anger. Addressing the crow, whom he could not see, he said, 'You monster, why have you come in the way of my coronation? What harm had I done you? From this day there is bitter enmity between your race and mine. The wound that you have caused will never heal.'

When the owl went away the crow reflected: 'Alas! I have unnecessarily made an enemy. That was foolish of me. One must never make an enemy for nothing, even if he is harmless. After all, we do not take poison just because there is a doctor in the locality. However, what is done is done.' And with these thoughts the crow left the spot, carrying vague apprehensions in his mind.

* * *

When Sthirajivi had finished his narrative of the ancient quarrel between owls and crows, Meghavarna said, 'Father, I now understand the deep-rooted enmity between the owls and ourselves. Our struggle is going to be a bitter one. Now what would you advise me to do?'

Sthirajivi answered, 'However difficult the circumstances, there is always an effective procedure to lead us to victory. We must not be tied up by the five classical expedients which my young friends have advocated one by one. What we need is to throw the enemy off his guard and to mislead him completely. When the three vagabonds deceived the Brahmin and grabbed his goat, they demonstrated how an unorthodox device may be used with success.'

Meghavarna said, 'I have not heard the story of the Brahmin and the vagabonds.'

So Sthirajivi told him this story.

THREE ROGUES
AND A BRAHMIN

There was once a Brahmin named Mitrasharma who was in charge of the sacred fire in a certain town. One day, when it was cold and the sky was overcast with clouds, he had to go to another village in order to procure a victim for the sacrifice. Having secured a nice, fat goat the Brahmin turned his footsteps homeward.

On the road he was seen by three vagabonds who had gone without food for some time. When they saw the goat flung upon the Brahmin's shoulders, their mouths watered. They whispered together, 'If only we could get hold of that creature! Why, we could have a fine hot roast! And what a pleasure that would be on a chilly afternoon like this.'

The rogues hit upon a plan to deprive the Brahmin of his goat.

One of them changed his dress and, overtaking the Brahmin by a shortcut, addressed him thus: 'Oh holy man, what has happened to you? Why are you carrying this dog on your shoulder? Don't you know that the dog is universally regarded as an unclean animal?'

The Brahmin was as furious as he was surprised. 'My man,' he said sharply, 'are you blind? You seem to have two clear eyes and yet attribute doghood to a goat!'

The rogue put on an ironical expression and said, 'Sir, you are right and I am wrong. It is indeed a goat. Do not be angry with me.'

When the Brahmin had proceeded a little farther, he was accosted by the second rascal, who said in a shocked voice, 'Alas, what are things coming to! The very idea of carrying a dead calf on one's shoulder! What sacrilege for a Brahmin! Sir, it is possible that the calf was a pet. I can understand your love for it. But after all there are certain things that are just not done. Now please purify yourself with a fast and perform charities.'

The Brahmin said angrily, 'Why, there is no end to blind men in this region. Stupid fellow, why do you call a goat a calf?'

'Holy Brahmin, calm yourself' said the scoundrel. 'Indeed, you are wise and I am ignorant even though you do put a dead calf on your shoulder. Please do whatever you please.'

By this time the Brahmin was in a thoroughly bad temper and his mind was confused. When, therefore, he met the third rogue, who accosted him as the others had done, he was no longer sure of himself. The rogue said, 'Sir, it is no business of mine, and yet I cannot keep silent when I see a Brahmin carrying a donkey on his shoulder. For a man of the highest caste it is a sin to touch a donkey. And if he does so by mistake, he must wash himself and do penance. Good lord, what an evil age we are living in!'

At this the Brahmin was convinced that what was given to him as a goat was really an evil spirit which had assumed the forms of different animals from time to time. So he threw the goat on the ground and fled in panic. The three rogues met, got hold of the goat, and had a rollicking good supper.

* * *

Sthirajivi continued, 'That is why I feel confident that through a clever device we shall gain our end. In fact I have already thought of something. But it is a plan that must be treated as a closely guarded secret.'

'Tell me what you have in mind,' said Meghavarna, whose curiosity was roused by the wise counsellor's words. 'We shall all be most circumspect.'

Sthirajivi said, 'Listen carefully, my son. You know the classical types of strategy based on conciliation, intrigue, bribery and assault. But I have hit upon an entirely new plan. We must stage a mock civil war and thus deceive the enemy. You shall pretend to turn against me, abuse me most cruelly and smear me with blood. Then you shall throw me at the foot of this tree and go away to a distant place. You must stay there with your followers until I win the enemy's trust and discover their secret castle. You should not feel any pity for me, though I know it will be difficult for you to treat me harshly even to hoodwink the enemy.'

The plan was carried out. Sthirajivi and Meghavarna staged a sham fight at a time when enemy spies were watching. Sthirajivi used rebellious language and insulted the king. The younger counsellors were enraged and were about to strike down Sthirajivi when the king intervened and said, 'You keep out of this, my friends. I shall personally punish this traitor.' And then he pounced upon the elder statesman, pecked at him, and smeared him with blood which he had already procured. Then, while Sthirajivi groaned and appeared to be at death's door, Meghavarna went away to a distant tree among the mountains.

As anticipated, spies reported the incident to the king of owls. At sundown Arimardana came to the banyan tree along with a few picked followers. He found that the enemy's headquarters were deserted. Arimardana gloated over his victory and court poets who were among the followers recited paeans of victory. The king said, 'Discover their line of retreat. We must pursue and destroy them before they make a new home.'

At this, Sthirajivi cawed in a feeble voice and attracted the attention of the owls. 'They were about to kill him when he said, 'Gentlemen, I am Meghavarna's minister. My name is Sthirajivi. You can see what reward I have obtained for my lifelong devotion to the king of crows. He has insulted and wounded me. I am now determined to have my vengeance. Please take me to your king. I want to discuss certain matters with him.'

Hearing that a distinguished counsellor of the rival king had deserted, Arimardana approached Sthirajivi and said, 'Well, Sir, what is it that you want to discuss with me? And who has reduced you to this state?'

The wily crow said, 'Oh King, I shall tell you the whole story. Yesterday that fool of a Meghavarna, mad with anger at the sight of the crows that you had killed, started for your fortress. I tried to restrain him. I told him you were too strong for us and that we should humbly seek peace by paying you tribute and recognising your overlordship. Instead of listening to my advice, the king suspected me of treachery. His advisers egged him on and you see the result. Forgetting what I had done for his welfare, he mercilessly attacked me. Now all ties of loyalty are broken. I take shelter with you. I shall conduct you to his new home and help you in completely destroying the race of crows.'

Arimardana now took counsel with his own advisers. He first questioned Raktaksha, who was the senior most among them. 'My worthy Sir,' he said, 'you have heard this crow's story. Now tell me what is to be done.'

'Oh King,' said Raktaksha in an impatient tone, 'surely there is nothing to consider. He is an enemy. Kill him without hesitation.'

But the other advisers did not agree with this opinion. One of them said that it would be heartless to put to death a person who was begging for shelter. Another asserted that Sthirajivi would be a valuable source of information regarding the enemy's plans, resources and tactics. A third said that friendship between former enemies was not a rare thing, and that Sthirajivi might turn out to be a pleasant and interesting companion. In this way all of them, in the name of either sentiment or expediency, advised that Sthirajivi should be admitted as a friend and the maximum advantage should be taken of him. Arimardana accepted this advice.

Raktaksha, however, stuck to his view. He was convinced that a calamitous decision had been taken by his king. He bitterly said, 'Gentlemen, you have the satisfaction of having paved the way for your master's ruin. How gullible you all are! How easily has the enemy thrown dust in your eyes! Even now it is not too late. I beseech you to reconsider your decision.'

Sthirajivi was apprehensive that the scales might be turned against him. So he hypocritically said, 'Oh King, I am in a poor state. I am hardly in a position to help you, and yet you are so kind to me. Now please grant me one favour. Ask your followers to kindle a blazing fire for me.'

Raktaksha taunted him and said, 'Indeed, for what holy purpose do you wish to enter fire?'

Sthirajivi replied, 'I wish to be reborn as an owl so that in my next birth I may be of some service to your king.'

But the clever counsellor was not taken in. 'My dear Sir', he said, 'you are indeed a great diplomat. But I assure you, even if you are reborn as an owl you would still be loyal to the crows. The bonds of nature cannot be severed. The mouse-maiden could have married a magnificent bridegroom. But she chose a mouse all the same!'

Since none of them had heard of the mouse-maiden's marriage, Raktaksha told them this story.

THE MOUSE-MAIDEN'S WEDDING

On the bank of the river Ganga there was once a hermitage where holy men spent their time in meditation, sacred rites, and the study of the scriptures. They sustained themselves only with roots, bulbs and fruit. Their dress consisted of a loincloth made out of the bark of trees. They led a life of self-denial and purity.

The father of this hermitage was Yajnavalkya, the great sage. One day, as he was rinsing his mouth after a bath in the sacred river, a small female mouse dropped from a hawk's beak. The sage caught the poor thing in midair, laid her tenderly on a leaf, and repeated his bath, followed by a ceremony of purification. Then, through the miraculous power that he had gained by his austerities, Yajnavalkya transformed the female mouse into a girl and took her with him to his hermitage.

Addressing his wife, who was childless, the sage said, 'My dear, chance has brought this girl to our home. You must accept her as your daughter and look after her.' So the wife reared the girl with great affection and petted her so much that she became self-willed.

When the girl attained the age of twelve, Yajnavalkya's wife said, 'The time has come when this daughter of ours should be married.'

'You are right,' said the sage. 'A maiden must be wedded before she attains womanhood. If her parents allow the years to slip by, she may remain a spinster. And then, in order to avoid sin, the father may marry her off to any husband, good, bad or indifferent. We must find a suitable husband without delay, some one who would be worthy of our dear daughter; some one who has fame, good looks, knowledge and comes of a noble family.'

'But,' said Yajnavalkya's wife, 'can you think of such a perfect bridegroom?'

'Of course I can,' the sage asserted. 'I have led a holy life and I am not afraid of aiming high. I shall ask the Blessed Sun himself to marry our daughter.'

And so the holy sage sent for the Sun who came at once. 'Sir, why have you remembered me?' the Sun asked. Yajnavalkya said, 'My dear, here is my daughter. She is in every way worthy to be your wife. Will you marry her?'

The Sun agreed. So the sage turned towards his daughter and said, 'Here is the Blessed Sun, the lamp of the universe. How do you like him for a husband?'

To his surprise the girl turned down the proposal. 'Oh no, father,' she said. 'He is too hot. Please find some one better than he is.'

Yajnavalkya turned to the Sun and asked him whether there was any one superior to him. The Sun replied, 'Yes, the Cloud is greater than I am. He has the power to obscure me.'

So the sage sent for the Cloud and asked the girl whether she was satisfied with his choice. But the girl disapproved. 'He is black and nebulous,' she said. 'Please find some one more worthy of me.' The holy man asked the Cloud whether there was any one superior to him, and the cloud mentioned the Wind. So the Wind was summoned, but the girl complained that he was too fidgety and asked for a better husband.

'Oh Wind,' said Yajnavalkya, 'is there any one stronger than you?'

'Certainly,' said the Wind, 'the Mountain is stronger than me. Try as I might, I cannot shake him.' So the Mountain was called and offered to the girl as her bridegroom. But she refused. 'Oh father,' she complained, 'just see how rough he is, and how hard. Please give me to some one else.'

Yajnavalkya turned to the Mountain and asked, 'Oh Noble Mountain, is there any one superior to you?'

The Mountain thought for a while and then remarked, 'Well, perhaps I can say that mice are superior to me. All the time they are burrowing holes in my body.'

So the sage summoned a mouse and asked his daughter, 'Little girl, what do you say to *this* bridegroom?'

As soon as she saw the mouse the girl was thrilled. She quivered with pleasure, and felt that she had met her own kind. 'Oh father, what a fine husband you have found for me,' she said rapturously. 'Please turn me into a mouse and marry me to him. I shall keep house for him in a manner befitting the race of mice.'

So Yajnavalkya turned the girl into a mouse once again and married her off.

★ ★ ★

'That is why,' said Raktaksha, 'I am convinced that even if you are reborn as an owl, all your affection will be for the crows.' Then, turning to his own king, he once more pleaded for the destruction of Sthirajivi. But Arimardana did not listen to him.

The owls took the crow to their own fortress. On the way, Sthirajivi laughed inwardly and said to himself: 'What fools these owls are. If they had any sense they would have listened to the sound advice given by Raktaksha. It is lucky for me that they have failed to see the wisdom of his words.'

When they came to the gate of the fortress, King Arimardana said, 'My friends, give our guest whichever room he prefers. He is our well-wisher.' When Sthirajivi heard this, he reflected: 'I must not stay inside the fortress. If I live among them, my movements would be watched and my true purpose betrayed.' So he said to the king of owls, 'Your Majesty, I am indeed your well-wisher. And I am touched by your kindness. But I know that a servant must stick to his own proper position. I shall take my place humbly at the fortress-gate, and every day I shall come to pay homage at your feet.'

Arimardana was flattered and trusted Sthirajivi completely. He ordered the royal cooks to send choice morsels of food to the guest every day. Very soon the wily crow became plump and vigorous like a peacock.

Meanwhile Raktaksha watched with amazement and anger the hospitality that was being lavished on an enemy. He repeated his warnings, but, since evil destiny had clouded the vision of Arimardana, his words were not heeded. So Raktaksha got together his own personal followers and said, 'My friends, it is now clear that the end of our race is in sight. As an ancestral counsellor it was my duty to have warned the king against the ruinous course that he is following. I have tried to save him, but I have failed. Now we have no further obligations. Let us seek another home.'

And so, bidding farewell to the fortress with heavy hearts, Raktaksha and his adherents departed in search of a new home.

Sthirajivi was overjoyed. 'The greatest obstacle in the way of my success is gone,' he reflected. 'Of all my enemies he alone was intelligent. All the others are stupid. My task is now easy. The classical writers have shown with many historical references that in the absence of farsighted advisers the downfall of a king is swift and certain.'

Day after day Sthirajivi felt more and more sure of himself. Gradually he began to collect a pile of faggots in his own dwelling near the gate of the fortress. The owls were too foolish to realize what he was doing. When sufficient wood had been piled up, Sthirajivi hastened to inform Meghavarna of his strategy. 'My son,' he said, 'everything is ready. You should now come with all your followers, each carrying a lighted faggot in his beak. Then let all these torches be simultaneously thrown upon my nest at the gate of the enemy's fortress. You will soon see the owls enduring the torments of hell.'

Meghavarna was delighted. 'Father, we are meeting after a long time,' he said. 'First tell me of your adventures.'

But the wise counsellor cut him short. 'This is no time for gossip,' he said. 'Some enemy spy might get wind of my plan. The enemy, though blind, may escape at the last moment. Let us not tarry a moment longer. When our victory is complete, I shall tell you the whole story.'

So Meghavarna and his followers flew to the enemy's fortress carrying lighted torches in their beaks. Then they set fire to the pile of wood which Sthirajivi had collected. The owls, being blind in the day time, saw nothing of what was being done. Soon the fire blazed furiously and, since there was no other exit, all the owls were burnt to death. Meghavarna returned to his old home in the banyan tree, and all the crows celebrated their victory over the ancestral foe.

When the festivities were over, Sthirajivi said, 'The strategy adopted by me in dealing with the owls yields us important lessons. It shows us that in the face of danger we must seek a path of escape, but should always have the ultimate object clearly in mind. We should be prudent even when we are optimistic. We must wait on fortune, watch our steps and curb our impetuosity.'

Meghavarna said, 'Father, your self-imposed task was difficult indeed. To live among the enemy is like submitting to the ordeal of the sword.'

'So it is,' said Sthirajivi. 'But my task was lightened because the enemies were so stupid. Never have I seen such a pack of fools anywhere else. Only Raktaksha was wise; his intellect was not blunted by his theoretical knowledge. He understood my tricks. But the other advisers were merely making a living in their king's service without giving anything in return. They did not know the most elementary principle of politics, namely, 'Never trust an enemy'. In associating with the owls I had to endure humiliation. I had to pose as a deserter and swear loyalty to their king. But all this is justifiable. The only important thing is to achieve the object. Even the big, black snake allowed frogs to ride upon his body. But he had a good laugh at the end.'

Meghavarna said that he had never heard the story of the snake and the frogs. So Sthirajivi narrated the following story.

THE CUNNING SNAKE

There was once a black snake named Mandavisha. He was so cunning that as long as he had physical strength he never lacked food. But in his old age he began to find it difficult to secure his victims. One day, desiring to get along without exertion, he thought out a plan.

He slowly approached a pond containing many frogs and remained seated on the bank with a sorrowful expression. After a while one of the frogs, who had been watching the snake for some time, timidly peeped out of the pond and said, 'Uncle, why are you so quiet today? Why don't you chase us? Are you not hungry?'

Mandavisha said, 'My friend, I have lost my desire for food. Yesterday I saw a frog and tried to catch him. He fled from me and escaped among a group of Brahmins who were reciting the scriptures. I looked for him among them and ultimately bit the toe of a Brahmin boy, mistaking it for a frog. The boy died at once, and his father cursed me. 'You monster,' he said, 'since you have caused the death of my poor little son you shall be punished. From this moment you shall become the vehicle of frogs. They will ride upon you and you will have to carry them wherever they please, subsisting on whatever food they give you out of pity.' That is why I have come here to serve as your vehicle.'

The frog went and reported this to his king, whose name was Jalapada. There was great rejoicing among the frogs. One by one they came out of the pond, led by Jalapada, and approached the snake. Mandavisha lay flat on the ground and invited the king of frogs to mount upon his hood. The king was joined by some of his advisers, and then by some of the soldiers. At last every spot of the snake's body was covered and he took the frogs for a joyride. Those who had failed to find a place on the snake's body hopped along behind him, clapping and shouting. Mandavisha showed them many interesting places and brought them back. Jalapada was in high spirits. 'I would rather ride this snake,' he said, 'than the finest horse, the most richly caparisoned elephant, or the most comfortable man-borne palanquin.'

The sport continued for a few days and then Mandavisha began to slacken. He would move slowly and soon get exhausted. Jalapada, who had got used to the fun, said, 'What is all this? Why don't you carry us cheerfully as before?'

Mandavisha replied, 'Oh King, the fact is that I am famished. I have no energy left.'

At this the king of frogs picked out some of his subjects and offered them to Mandavisha for his supper. The cunning snake remarked, 'The Brahmin's curse has now come true in every respect. He had ordained that I would have to subsist on your charity. Now I can serve you as before.' And so he again began to take the king out for joyrides.

Jalapada, determined to indulge in this amusement at any cost, went on offering to the snake frog after frog. And at last, when all his subjects were gobbled up, the snake promptly caught hold of the king himself and made a meal of him.

Thus Mandavisha, by feigning subservience, attained his purpose.

* * *

Sthirajivi continued, 'From this story, my son, it becomes apparent that to enter the enemy's camp, and even to serve the enemy for a while, can prove a valuable artifice. That is why I lived among the owls and pretended to be loyal to their king.

Our war against the owls is now over. You are fortunate. May you continue to enjoy the pleasures of kingship with prudence, self-sacrifice and courage. Our scriptures have laid down that association with the wise leads to virtue; virtue leads to wealth; wealth is the prelude to fame; fame brings power and authority; and these signify the fulfillment of real purpose.'

Meghavarna was deeply moved by his counsellor's words. He expressed his gratitude and said, 'Father, all this is the reward of your thorough knowledge of political economy, ethics and military science. With what wonderful acumen did you penetrate the fortress of the owls and exterminate Arimardana and his band!'

'It is true I had a measure of success,' said Sthirajivi. 'Remember, extreme steps should never be taken immediately; they should always be preceded by subtle devices. Sometimes gentleness is a necessary preparation for aggression. When a man is about to fell a mighty tree, he first utters a prayer.

My heart is now at peace. I have seen the undertaking through. I wish your dynasty glory and splendour through a long succession of sons, grandsons and beyond. But be careful not to be intoxicated by success or grandeur. The power of kings is transitory, like everything else. Royal glory is difficult to climb, like a bamboo; it is hard to hold, being fidgety like a monkey on a treetop; it is balanced precariously, like drops of water on a lotus-leaf; it is changeable, like the path of the wind; it is undependable, like the friendship of a dishonest man; it is difficult to tame, like a serpent; it glistens only for a moment, like a cloud at sunset; it is fragile, like bubbles on the surface of a river; it is elusive, like the treasure attained in a dream. Remember all this, and enjoy your kingdom modestly.'

Meghavarna took the wise counsellor's words to heart and, ruling with justice and humility, enjoyed the pleasures of royalty for a long, long time.

KADAMBARI

·

BANABHATTA

Banabhatta's *fame rests on two works:* Harshacharita, *a laudatory account of his patron, King Harshavardhana, and* Kadambari, *which has come to represent the very essence of the story-teller's art, so much so that the word 'kadambari' is itself often used in the sense of 'a novel'.*

Harshavardhana died in 648 A.D., *and it is known that* Kadambari *was composed in the last years of his reign, if not after his death. The literary activity of Banabhatta can therefore be assigned to the middle decades of the seventh century.*

The plot of Kadambari *is exceedingly complicated and involved. Long narratives are interrupted by flashbacks, and these lead to still longer narratives. There are endless digressions, and the major portion of the story is put in a parrot's mouth. It has been rightly objected that 'no reader can carry in his head a figment of this kind through a romance of four hundred pages.'*

But all these shortcomings are readily forgiven when we think of Banabhatta's brilliant descriptions, his picturesque imagery, his lively imagination, his beautifully worked out metaphors and his deep sensitiveness to the life of nature. He handles his characters with great skill. Even the minor figures are lively and consistent. They fill their roles with perfect naturalness, and their presence never appears superfluous.

Banabhatta's *sympathies are broad. He shows profound understanding of the human emotions, and especially of the joys and tribulations that spring from love. His treatment of love is free from the remotest suggestion of anything that might be considered gross or coarse. In* Kadambari, *the emphasis is always placed on the finer and the more ennobling aspects of love. Mahashweta's passion has a flame-like purity; and her sorrow a cleansing power, that prepare the reader psychologically for the appearance of the heroine. And when the princess of the* Gandharvas *arrives on the scene, she brings with her a freshness, a tenderness and a spontaneous grace that are utterly disarming.*

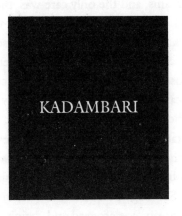

KADAMBARI

There was once a great king named Shudraka who rose in fresh splendour every day, like the sun. He was an upholder of the moral law and never failed to offer sacrifices whenever they were due. He was the source of all the arts and the home of all virtue. He was the ambrosial spring of poesy. To his friends he was like the sunrise, but to his foes he was a dire comet. All men of taste found in him a ready ally. But the haughty cut no ice with him.

In his reign banners alone trembled, and songs alone showed variations. The only fetters were the fetters of prosody, the only deception was in dreams, and the only care was that concerning good conduct. Elephants alone were rampant, lattice-windows alone had ensnaring meshwork. Shudraka's subjects never deserted their homes— though, of course, chessmen had to leave their empty squares! The only tears were those caused by the smoke of sacrificial fire, and the sound of the lash came only when horses were whipped into speed.

One day, as the king sat in his audience-hall, a female messenger approached him gracefully and, placing her knees humbly upon the ground, said, 'Sir, there is at the palace-gate a *Chandala* maiden from the south. She has brought with her a parrot which she claims to be a veritable marvel. She begs permission to present the bird to you.'

The king's curiosity was aroused and, being in a leisurely mood, he said, 'Why not? Let her be admitted.' Very soon the *Chandala* maiden was ushered into the royal presence. She saw the king surrounded by a thousand chieftains, like golden-peaked Meru surrounded by lesser Himalayan snowpeaks. He sat on a couch encrusted with moonstones. Above him was a silken canopy, white like the foam of the heavenly river. Its jewelled pillars were kept together by chains of gold, entwined with strings of pearls. His left foot rested on a footstool of crystal, as if the moon had bent down in humiliation before the beauty of his countenance. His limbs were tinged with blue from the reflected light of the sapphire pavement, as if darkened by the sighs of his defeated enemies.

The *Chandala* maiden was for a moment overwhelmed by the king's splendid appearance. Then she advanced with tinkling bracelets and struck the mosaic floor with her staff. She was accompanied by a man hoary with age and yet strong in every limb. Behind them was a *Chandala* boy with long hair falling on each shoulder. He carried a parrot in a cage, and although the bars of the cage were made of gold they shone like emerald through the reflection of the parrot's plumage. The maiden was dressed in a blue garment which reached down to

her ankle, and wore a veil of red silks—a combination glorious like
the evening sunshine falling on a pool of blue lotuses. Her white
earrings were suspended on her dark cheeks, as if the face of Night
were adorned by the rays of the rising moon. She had reached the
flower of her youth and was at the height of beauty. The king reflected
in amazement: 'The Creator's ways are indeed beyond prediction! With
a form that scorns the accumulated loveliness of the Universe, why
was she born in a *Chandala* race?'

While the king was thus wrapped in wonder, the maiden stepped
on the mosaic floor and made a sign to her attendant who pointed to
the parrot and said, 'Sir, here is Vaishampayana, the parrot, who knows
the meaning of all the *Shastras* and who is well versed in royal policy,
history and mythology. He has a perfect command over musical
intervals. He recites poems and narrates romances composed by himself.
His witticisms will hold you spellbound. He can play on the *Veena*,
the flute and the drum. He is familiar with the characteristics of
elephants, horses and other animals. He knows all the movements of
classical dance, has a perfect knowledge of histrionics, and is a skilful
painter. He even knows how to pacify a maiden's anger in a love-
quarrel. Oh King, all gems belong naturally to you, as the pearls belong
to the ocean. That is why this maiden, who is the daughter of the
king of *Chandalas,* has brought Vaishampayana to you as a gift. Pray
accept it and gratify us.'

The attendant placed the cage before the king and retired. The
parrot raised his right foot, hailed the king, and recited a song of his
own composition. The king turned in amazement towards his minister,
Kumarapalita, and said, 'Counsellor, did you hear the bird's clear
rendering of consonants? Did you mark the sweetness and grace of
his intonation? Never have I witnessed a marvel to compare with this.
Such a combination of correctness and elegance may well be the envy
of the most accomplished poets and musicians.'

While the king was praising the parrot in this way, the mid-day conch sounded. The king dismissed all his courtiers. The hour of bathing was at hand. The sound of anklets was heard on all sides as fan-bearers and other female attendants hastily left the audience-hall. The king ordered Vaishampayana to be taken into the inner apartments and proceeded to the bathing pavilion.

When he laid aside his ornaments, it seemed as if the sun had divested itself of its rays, or the sky 'had become bare of moon and stars. Having taken pleasant exercise for a while he entered the bathing place. It had a gold bath filled with perfumed water. A crystal bathing-seat was placed by its side. Beautifully decorated pitchers stood on one side, full of fragrant water. Some of the handmaidens held small silver pitchers in their hands and poured out fresh perfumes. Bards sang appropriate songs in the background. Musicians played on various instruments. The king bathed, dressed in a robe of fine silk, and was anointed with sandalwood paste. Then, having partaken of a light meal and taken his betel, he entered his chamber. He reclined on a couch and conversed with his intimate companions.

After a while, curious to learn the parrot's story, he sent for Vaishampayana. When the bird was brought into his presence the king asked him, 'Well, my dear fellow, have you been properly fed and bathed? Is everything to your taste?' The parrot replied, 'Your Majesty, what have I not eaten! I have had my fill of the juice of *jambu* fruits. I have cracked the seeds of blood-red pomegranates. I have pecked at grapes and played with lotus shoots. But is it necessary to describe the delicacies that I have tasted? Everything touched by the hands of your beautiful queens turns into ambrosia.'

The king cut him short and said, 'Enough of all this. Now tell me of your birth and adventures, your parentage and education. I am eager to know all about you. How did you come to acquire such deep knowledge of the scriptures? Are you dwelling in disguise or is this your true form? And how did you fall into the hands of a *Chandala* maiden? Tell me everything.'

Vaishampayana said, 'Sir, the story is a long one. But, if such be your pleasure, hear it.' And then the parrot narrated the history of his former life.

II

In the region of the Vindhya mountains there is a forest abounding in beautiful trees, damp with the ichor of wild elephants. Its bowers are dark and shady; and its pools are full to the brim with cool water.

In this forest, not far from the hermitage of sage Agastya, there is a lotus-lake called Pampa. It is like a second ocean made by the Creator as the home of all that is peerless. On the bank of this lake, near a clump of palms, there is a large silk-cotton tree. Its roots are always encircled by an ancient snake as by the trunk of a mighty elephant. Its countless branches, spreading through the firmament, seem to imitate the thousand arms of Siva, outstretched in his wild dance. Through the weight of its years the tree seems to lean for support on the shoulder of the wind. The creepers that cling to its trunk stand out like the swollen veins of old age. On the topmost branches of this tree there are wisps of cotton which look like the foam dripping from the panting mouths of the sun's horses. This tree is like a temple from where the gods of the forest look out upon the Universe.

In this tree thousands of parrots had once made their homes. They had settled upon the boughs, in the crevices, in the holes of the rotting bark and among the hollows. Concealed by the dense foliage of this lord of the forest, the parrots lived peacefully. They spent the nights in their own nests and at dawn formed delightful lines in the sky. When the flock was on the wing, it seemed like a moving floor of emeralds. Their progress in the sky seemed to fashion a grassy path stretching through to heaven. After gathering their food they returned to their young ones, their beaks dripping with the juice of fruits.

In one of the old hollows of this tree my parents, too, had made their dwelling. Fate decreed that I should be an only child and, to my father's everlasting sorrow, my mother lost her life in the pains of childbirth. My father devoted himself wholly to my nurture. Owing to his advanced age, his wings had lost their power of flight and hung loose from his shoulders. When he shook them, it seemed that he was trying to shake off the painful old age that clung to his body. He was unable to wander far, and had to content himself with bits of fruit torn down by other parrots. Now and again he picked up grains of rice fallen from other nests, with a beak worn thin through a lifetime of effort in breaking the hard seeds of various fruits. He could collect very little, and subsisted on whatever was left over after feeding me.

One day I suddenly heard the tumult of a hunting expedition. The night was nearing its end. The moon, like an old swan with its wings reddened by lotus honey, had descended to the shore of the western ocean. The lions were yawning. Inspired by the flapping of the elephants' ears, the peacocks were beginning to dance. The sun had risen and was playing among the treetops around the Pampa lake. Groups of parrots had already left the tree in search of food. My father was still in his own nest and I nestled close to him. At that moment the sound of the chase descended upon us like a thunderbolt. It terrified every creature of the forest and was soon mingled with the shrieks of frightened elephants. By and by the noise was swollen by the roar of lions wakened from their sleep in mountain caves. The entire forest trembled as the hunters shouted to each other and pursued the fleeing beasts. The deer cried piteously as their young ones were torn by the hounds from limb to limb. Birds circled overhead in confusion uttering strange sounds, while woodland nymphs fled in terror.

As the tumult slowly subsided I plucked up courage and peeped out of the tree-trunk. I saw an army of *shabaras* filling the forest with their awesome forms. It was as though all the nights of the dark fortnight had been rolled into one; as though all the curses uttered by angry hermits had congealed into bodily form; as though a huge mass of black clouds upon a mountain-peak had been suddenly broken into bits by a terrific blow from a lion's paw. The *shabaras* numbered many thousands and the earth was darkened by their advance.

At the head of this great army I saw their leader, Matanga. Though still in his early youth, he was hard as if made of iron. He had a well-grown beard and his thick curly locks hung upon his shoulders like a lion's mane. He was broad of brow, stern of nose. His left side shone with the rays of a jewelled snake's hood with which he had adorned one of his ears. He seemed to dye the steps with his bloodshot eyes, as though shedding a twilight of doom for all living creatures. His mighty arms reached down to his knees: they seemed to have been made to the measure of an elephant's trunk. His legs were strong, his shoulders rough with scars. He was accompanied by hounds of every colour. Their lolling tongues, though dry with fatigue, seemed by their natural pinkness to be dripping with the blood of deer. These hounds were trained in the art of initiating does into the state of widowhood.

Matanga was followed by *shabaras*, some of whom carried tiger-skins. Others held peacocks' tails; still others flaunted elephant-tusks. When I saw this mighty army, I reflected: 'The life of these men is full of folly, and their career utterly blameworthy. Their only religion is the offering of human flesh to Durga. Hunting is their only exercise, the cry of the jackal is their only *Shastra*. Dogs are their bosom friends; their feast is a drinking bout; their kingdom is in weird and deserted places and their wives are captives taken in battles. Their livelihood is by theft and cruelty, and the hoods of snakes are their only ornaments.'

As I was thinking in this manner Matanga approached the very tree in which we had our home. He sat down under the tree on a seat of twigs hastily made ready by his servants. He was served with freshly plucked lotus-fibres which he devoured greedily. After he had eaten he drank the cool, aromatic water fetched from the lake by one of his followers. Matanga rested for a while and then, rising with fresh energy, continued his progress through the forest along with his followers.

But one of the *shabaras* lingered on. Apparently he had gone without his share of deer-flesh and his demoniac expression proclaimed his desire for meat. As soon as others had vanished from sight this barbarian looked up at the tree and his mouth watered at the sight of so many parrots. He reckoned up the number of nests in the tree and chuckled at the thought of the destruction he was about to wreak. Then he started climbing the tree without the slightest difficulty. He grabbed the young parrots from the boughs one by one as if they were fruit. Some were only a few days old, others were newborn babes that looked like cotton flowers, still others, with their wings just sprouting, were like fresh lotus-leaves. He pitilessly slew them all and cast them upon the ground.

My father trembled at the destruction that he saw. His limbs quivered and his eyes were vacant through fear of death. His palate was dry and his joints paralysed. He covered me with his wings and held me to his breast. Slowly that brute of a *shabara* approached our nest and thrust his left arm inside. It was dreadful like the body of an old black snake, and redolent with the raw fat of a wild boar that he had slain. My father struck out helplessly with his beak and moaned piteously. But the murderous wretch dragged him down and crushed him. I was so small that my body was curled into a ball through fear and, concealed by my father's wings, I escaped the *shabara's* attention. He wrung my father's neck and threw him down. I slowly emerged from the shelter of my father's wings, protective even in death. Heartless wretch that I was, I saved myself instead of joining my father in the world beyond. I tottered along with the help of my feeble wings and came to the foot of a *tamala* tree. The *shabara* climbed down the tree, gathered up the parrots lying dead on the ground, packed them hastily in a basket of leaves, secured the basket with a coil of creepers, and went his way.

The craving for life is natural to all created beings. My life went on shamefully and, in spite of my consuming grief for my father's death, I longed for water to sustain my failing breath. The distant notes of the cranes told me that the lake was far away. My limbs were weary. I despaired of ever reaching the brink of water. But at that very moment a youthful hermit happened to pass that way. His countenance was so pure and bright that he seemed to have dropped from the rising sun. His limbs seemed to have been fashioned from lightning and his entire form painted with molten gold. He carried a bright crystal rosary, and a black antelope skin hung from his shoulders. In his right hand there was a staff on which was adjusted a leafy basket full of the flowers he had gathered for the worship of Siva. He was followed by a tame deer from the hermitage.

The ascetic noticed me and was filled with pity. He picked me up and carried me to the edge of the lake. Lifting my head, he made me drink a few drops of cool water. When I had recovered my breath he placed me in the life giving shade of a fresh lotus-leaf. Then he went through the ritual of bath and prayer. Having finished his oblations he donned a pure white robe, adjusted his topknot, and carried me to the hermitage where he lived.

In this hermitage Jabali, the great sage, had his *ashrama*. Young pupils were muttering Vedic hymns. The peacocks were hearing with delight the sound of the filling of pitchers. Parched grain was being scattered in the yards around the huts. The balls of rice offered to deities were being devoured by cocks of the forest. The aroma of half-cooked sacrificial cakes filled the atmosphere. The air was resonant with the cackle of fire-wood. Bark garments were being washed, lotus-seeds dried and fuel stacked for future use.

In this *ashrama* everything was pure and sacred. There was sharpness only in blades of grass, not in dispositions. There was wavering only among plantain leaves swaying in the wind, but there was no wavering in minds. Necks were clasped—but only of pitchers. Love of dance prevailed only among peacocks; monkeys alone showed a 'desire for fruit'; and only the roots of banyan trees had a downward tendency.

As I was admiring the hermitage, my eyes were purified by the sight of Jabali who sat in a quiet corner, surrounded by his disciples. I reflected: 'Happy is Goddess Saraswati who dwells in the serene mind of this sage. The depths of his soul are unfathomable. All the sciences become pure when they reach him, as the muddy rivers of the rainy season become pure when autumn arrives. The wind itself seems to approach him timidly and hardly disturbs the folds of his robe. The sage Jabali is a constant stream of sympathy, the bridge over the ocean of transitory existence, the reservoir of patience, the ocean of the nectar of contentment, the root of the tree of endurance, the rim of the wheel of wisdom. He is like an axe for the creepers of desire, the staff of the flag of virtue. He is like a potent charm against the snakes of anger and greed. Through the grace of this holy man the hermitage is free from envy and conflict. Here even the animals have abandoned their feuds. Here a snake, weary of basking in the sun, playfully enters a peacock's tail; and the peacock does not mind. Here a young antelope fearlessly plays about with tiger cubs. A lion closes his eyes and derives pleasure when his mane is pulled by young elephants who mistake it for lotus fibres. Here even the monkeys have shed their capriciousness: they dutifully gather fruits for the hermits. Why, even the trees, clad in bark and adorned with flowery garlands, look like fellow ascetics of this holy man.'

As I was lost in these reflections the hermit who had rescued me addressed the sage and said, 'Sir, I found this little parrot fallen from his nest. He was faint with heat and lay in the dust shaken by his fall. There was hardly any life left in him. As I could not replace him in his nest I have brought him here. Let him live with us while he is weak and unable to fly. We shall feed him on the juice of fruits and on tender grains of rice. When his wings are ready to take him into the open sky he will go where he pleases. But it is possible that, learning to love us, he may elect to stay on in this hermitage.'

Jabali heard these remarks and then directed his calm but penetrating glance at me. With his head bent slightly he gazed upon me as if trying to recognize me. After a while he said, 'He is only reaping the fruit of his own conduct.' At these words all the hermits, aware of his power and wisdom, became curious to know the history of my former birth. They said, 'Sir, please tell us what misconduct has brought upon this parrot all the suffering that he has endured. What was he in his former birth? We are eager to know about him.'

The saint replied, 'The story of this wonderful parrot is a long one. The day is almost over. The time of the evening prayer approaches. Later on, when you are resting quietly, I shall tell you the entire story from beginning to end. Meanwhile let some one attend to the poor bird. Let him be properly fed and housed.'

The glow of evening faded 'and gradually vanished. The sun glided from the sky, pink as a dove's foot. His orb, with its network of crimson rays, was now like the lotus of Vishnu, recumbent on his couch of water. Twilight sprang up like rosy coral from the western horizon. The hermitage became the home of quiet thought. The only sound heard was that of milking the cows. Making sure that the sun had gone to rest, the Lord of the Night, in pure serenity of light, wrapped in the whiteness of gossamer, made his appearance. When half a watch of the night was over the hermit who had picked me up, unable to restrain his eagerness any longer, went to Jabali again. Other hermits joined him in entreating the sage to relate the story of my former birth. And this is what Jabali said.

III

Who has not heard of Ujjayini, the proudest gem among all the cities of earth? Siva created it as a worthy abode for himself. Ujjayini is never enveloped in darkness, nor is there any need of lamps, so luminous are the jewels of its women. The home of splendour, the greatest glory of the golden age, the source of wealth and happiness, Ujjayini is indeed a marvel among human habitations.

In this city there was a great king named Tarapida who had conquered the earth by the might of his arm. He was wise and resolute, with an intellect ever devoted to study. His brilliance and glory made him a third luminary alongside the sun and the moon. From him proceeded all virtues like a flock of white swans emerging from the Himalayan snowlands. While he ruled, truth was secure and holy men received honour. None dared to face him except his own mirror. Nothing was eclipsed except the sun and the moon; nothing was dependent except the suffixes of compound words.

The king had a minister, Shukanasa by name, skilled in all the precepts of politics, the very castle of constancy. Shukanasa and the king were bound with ties of deep affection grown since the early years of childhood. After reigning happily for a few years Tarapida shifted the burdens of state to the shoulders of Shukanasa and gave himself up to a life of comfort and pleasure. There was, however, a source of great sorrow in his life. His queen, Vilsasavati, had borne him no progeny. She was the fairest ornament of his palace. She was to him what the shore is to the ocean, the creeper to the tree, lotus clusters to a lake, flowers to the spring and stars to the sky. Tarapida loved her

and, seeing her pine for a child, was himself weighed down by gloom.
One day he saw her seated on a couch weeping bitterly, surrounded by her companions, also mute in grief. Her silken garment was wet with tears, her tresses were in disorder. The king exclaimed in an anxious voice: 'My Queen, why this weeping, voiceless and heavy with oppression? Why are your eyelashes stringing a net of pearls? Why are your jewelled anklets deprived of the touch of your feet? Have I done any wrong, or has any of the attendants failed in his duty towards you?'

The queen was silent, but one of her companions plucked up courage to say: 'My Lord, how could any wrong, however trifling, proceed from you? And how could any one dare to offend your queen? For a long time she has grieved because her marriage has not proved fruitful. She tries to conceal her sorrow, but today she heard in the temple a verse from the scriptures which says: 'No bright future awaits those deprived of progeny. A son alone can deliver the parents from darkness.' Ever since she heard these words she is inconsolable. We have failed to soothe her.'

The king tried to cheer her as best as he could. He reminded her that it was not for mortals to question the decrees of fate. He exhorted her to redouble her attention to the gods and the *gurus*; to be ever more mindful of the laws of hospitality and duty. From that time onward Vilasavati became more and more devoted to the propitiation of gods. She honoured the Brahmins, paid reverence to all holy persons and redoubled her charities. She bathed in all the renowned snake-ponds of the kingdom, worshipped all the sacred trees, and paid homage to wandering ascetics. She invited reciters of holy books to her palace and imbibed all the lessons of the epics. She honoured the fortune-tellers, and with her own hands made offerings of grains of rice to the birds who visited her terraces. She tied strings of medicinal herbs to her arms as amulets.

A few days passed. Then one night, when the sky was gray like
the wings of an aging pigeon, and when the stars were taking their
leave one by one, King Tarapida had a wonderful dream. He saw the
full moon entering the mouth of Vilasavati like a ball of lotus fibres
going into an elephant's trunk. As soon as he woke up he called
Shukanasa and described what he had seen. The minister was filled
with joy and said, 'Your Majesty, our wishes are about to be fulfilled.
I, too, have seen a dream a few moments ago. It seemed to me that a
white-robed Brahmin, godlike of bearing and serene of aspect, placed
in the lap of my wife, Manorama, a wonderful lotus dripping with
honey. These auspicious omens seen by us are harbingers of happiness.
You will get a son, a leader among all the royal sages that have ever
appeared upon the earth. And he will gladden your heart as the lotus-
pool in autumn gladdens the royal elephant.'

Shukanasa's words came true. In course of time Vilasavati gave
birth to a son. The king, commemorating the dream in which the
moon had appeared, gave to the prince the name of Chandrapida.
Shukanasa's wife, Manorama, also delivered a son. He was named
Vaishampayana.

IV

Chandrapida and Vaishampayana grew up together. All the ceremonies
appropriate to childhood were performed by their parents with due
regard to religion. When the time came to initiate the prince into the
life of scholarship, King Tarapida had a Palace of Learning built outside
the city. It stretched half a league along the river. It was surrounded
by a wall of white marble, with a great moat running outside. It was
provided with stables for horses and sheds for palanquins. A gymnasium
was constructed and placed in charge of renowned athletes. In this
Palace of Learning the king brought together teachers of every science,

and Chandrapida was placed under their care. He was like a young lion in a cage, with every allurement removed and with his mind free from every distraction.

The prince began to acquire knowledge of all the *Shastras.* The efforts of his teachers were quickened by his own great powers. The whole range of arts and sciences assembled in his mind as in a pure jewelled mirror. He acquired the highest skill in grammar, law, prosody and diplomacy. He learned to handle the bow, the scimitar, the shield, the battle-axe and other weapons. He mastered the laws of dance and music laid down by Bharata and other teachers of antiquity. He acquired dexterity in painting, calligraphy, testing of jewels, working in ivory and playing upon cymbal, lute, pipe and other instruments. He learnt architecture, engineering and mechanics. He became familiar with foreign languages, and was thoroughly initiated into the epics, the scriptures, ancient chronicles, narrative poems and drama.

Along with these mental disciplines he also acquired great physical prowess. When he playfully pulled the ears of young elephants their limbs shook through the weight of his muscles. With a single stroke of his scimitar he could cut down full-grown palm-trees as if they were lotus stalks. For his exercise he used an iron club which could only be lifted by ten men.

Vaishampayana also progressed in body and mind and became a close second to his royal companion. The two became inseparable and there was absolute confidence between them. Chandrapida could not do without Vaishampayana for a moment, and the latter followed him ceaselessly as the day follows the sun. Chandrapida's limbs acquired fullness, like the wishes of his friends; his waist became slender, like the armies of rival kings; his form broadened, like his liberality; his majesty grew, like his hair; his eyes became bright, like his conduct; and his heart became deep, like his own voice.

When the prince's education was complete King Tarapida sent one of his trusted counsellors, Balahaka, with this message: 'My son, you have fulfilled all our hopes. You have studied the *Shastras*, mastered the sciences and perfected the arts. Your teachers report that you are fit to leave the house of learning. Now let people see you like a royal elephant emerging from the enclosure. You are in the sixteenth year of your life. Come out and gratify the eyes of the world. Pay your respects to all the chiefs of the kingdom, do honour to the Brahmins and protect your people. I send you a horse worthy to bear your weight. This horse, Indrayudha by name, is swift like Garuda, the king of eagles. He is tireless like the wind. The emperor of Persia has sent him to me as a gift. Ride this horse, my son, and come back to the city.'

When Balahaka had delivered this message, Prince Chandrapida bowed his head as a mark of respect for his father's command, and said, 'Let Indrayudha be brought to me. 1 am eager to mount him.' Very soon that wonderful steed was led into his presence. Two men grasped the bit on each side in an effort to curb Indrayudha's energy. The horse was so large that his back was just within reach of a man's uplifted hands. He snorted in wrath at any hindrance to his course. He seemed to be examining the three worlds as if making ready to leap over them. His body was streaked with yellow, green and pink so that he resembled a rainbow. Flakes of foam spouted from his frothing lips.

Chandrapida looked at the horse in amazement. 'What a jewel!' he exclaimed. 'What has Indra, the lord of all the gods, gained by his mastery of the three worlds if he has not mounted this horse? My father's royal glory must surely surpass all the riches of heaven if he has such treasures as this. Noble Indrayudha, I hail you. Forgive my audacity in mounting you.'

As if understanding every syllable, the horse looked at him

steadily. His eyes blinked as he tossed his mane and repeatedly struck the ground with his right hoof. The hair on his chest was tinged with gray as it was covered by the dust raised by his hoofs. He uttered a pleasant whinnying sound as if summoning the prince to ride him. Chandrapida seated himself firmly on his back and emerged from the gate of the house of learning. He saw a mighty cavalcade assembled to welcome him. The clatter of hoofs seemed to fill the hollows of earth and heaven. At Chandrapida's approach all the riders were in motion, like waves at the rising of the moon. Balahaka presented the princes and the nobles of the realm one by one. They bent their heads respectfully and Chandrapida acknowledged their homage. A large umbrella with a golden stick was borne above him during the ceremony: it was like the lotus on which his glory might dwell. A thousand voices cheered him and wished him long life and victory.

Accompanied by Vaishampayana, the prince rode through the streets of Ujjayini. Windows on the balconies were hastily opened. Women left their work half-done. Some of them, their hands freshly painted with henna, were like lotus-buds in early sunlight. Others, whose tender feet were enmeshed in the bells of their girdles, moved slowly, like elephants restrained by their chains. When these beauties appeared at the emerald-studded lattices and gazed upon the prince, it seemed as though an entire grove had blossomed out at once. The city seemed girt by the stream of their charms. The sky seemed studded with innumerable moons. Chandrapida's lovely form entered into their hearts as if they were mirrors. Their graceful speech was marked by witty remarks, tender confidences, mutual coquettishness, confusion, coyness, and longing. Some of them were absentminded, others lost in curiosity, still others inquisitive. Some tried naughtily to attract the prince's attention, others were angry because the prince directed his glance at someone else.

Meanwhile Chandrapida continued his progress. The crest of jasmine flowers under his umbrella looked like a mass of moonbeams falling upon his dark hair which they had mistaken for the night. When he laughed as he exchanged remarks with Vaishampayana, the space between them was illumined by the brightness of his teeth. At last he reached the palace, passed through the crowd of attendant kings, and saw his father seated on a couch.

While the prince was still at some distance, the king rose from his couch and stretched his arms eagerly. His eyes were filled with tears of joy. At last he embraced his son as if he wanted to absorb him in his own body. Then he also embraced Vaishampayana and asked the two of them to go to the inner apartments. Chandrapida entered his mother's chamber and satisfied the claims of her affection. She embraced him repeatedly, and kissed his brow. After gazing upon him fondly for a while, queen Vilasavati said to her son, 'My child, your lather was indeed hard-hearted. He made you undergo such a severe training for so many years. How did you endure the tedious discipline imposed by your gurus? How have you acquired, with such tenderness of youth, the fortitude of a strong man?'

After spending some time with his mother Chandrapida mounted Indrayudha again and, accompanied by Vaishampayana, visited Shukanasa. He saluted the great counsellor as though he were a second father. Rejecting the jewelled seat brought for him, he sat respectfully on the bare ground. Shukanasa advanced towards him and, after looking into his eyes for a few moments, said, 'My child, King Tarapida has now truly gained his heart's desire. He has seen you grown to youth and possessed of all knowledge. The gods of your race are now content. Blessed are the subjects who will have you as their protector. Go, now, and help your father to carry the burden of the earth.' The prince listened to these words respectfully and then, entering the inner chamber, paid his homage to Vaishampayana's mother, Manorama.

Returning to his palace he found that a sacrifice to Agni was being performed. The gateways of the palace were decorated with white jars on either side. Green sandal branches hung above the pediments. Thousands of white flags fluttered in the air. Every one was dressed in bright clothes. In this way the round of festivities and ceremonies went on until the day came to a close.

Next morning Chandrapida mounted Indrayudha and went out on a hunt, accompanied by a retinue of runners, beaters, horses and elephants. Expert hunters held trained hounds in golden leashes. Chandrapida killed many lions, boars and other animals; while others he captured alive with great skill and courage. Woodland goddesses looked at him with half-closed eyes, frightened by the twanging of his bow. When the hunt was over he returned to his chamber and bathed with scented water stored in a hundred pitchers of gold and silver. He was anointed with sandal paste and perfumed with rare lotions. Then, putting on white raiment, he went to the banquet hall. A low table was covered with a hundred jewelled utensils and dishes. It looked like the autumn sky gleaming with the brightness of its stars. Chandrapida enjoyed his meal at leisure, conversing pleasantly with Vaishampayana.

Next day a messenger came from his mother, Queen Vilasavati, and said, 'Prince, I bring to you Patralekha, daughter of the king of Kuluta. Your mother has brought her up as her own daughter. She came as a captive when the royal city of Kuluta was captured by your father. The queen bids you take the greatest care of her. She will stay with you as your betel-bearer. You must shield her from the thoughtless and strive to make her happy. Such is your mother's wish.' Chandrapida accepted Patralekha in his train. From that moment she was filled with devotion for him and followed him like his shadow. The prince developed great affection for her and trusted her with all his secrets.

V

After a few days the king decided that Chandrapida should be anointed as the Crown Prince. When the preparations for the ceremony were completed, Shukanasa called the prince aside and gave him appropriate advice. 'Dear Chandrapida,' he said, 'you have learnt all the sciences, and read all the *Shastras*. But there is much that you have still to learn. The darkness arising from youth is very thick and cannot be pierced by the sun, nor by the radiance of all the jewels in the treasury. The intoxication of Lakshmi is terrible and does not leave us even in old age. The blindness of power admits of no cure. The fever of pride does not yield to any cooling appliances. The poison of the senses is maddening; no charms or medicinal herbs can counteract it. Passion leaves a stain that cannot be washed by bathing or purification.

In early youth the mind often loses its purity even though it is cleansed by knowledge of the scriptures. Nature carries a young heart before it like a dry leaf borne by the wind. The senses are captivated by pleasure, as deer are charmed by a mirage.

Beware of Lakshmi, my son. She is fickle and her ways are but little understood. When acquired she is hard to keep. Even though held fast by the cords of heroism, she escapes. Though guarded by elephants she flees away. She does not regard race, she does not follow the fortune of a family, does not consider character, does not count intelligence, does not court righteousness, does not honour generosity. She has no use for sacred learning, she does not understand truth, she does not value discrimination. Like the hazy outline of an aerial city, she vanishes as soon as we look upon her. She dwells on the edge of a sword, as if perpetually engaged in learning cruelty. Like a creeper, she is a parasite; like a river, she is full of bubbles; like the sun's rays on a cloudy day, she rests now on one thing and now on another. She regards the virtuous as impure, she despises the lofty as unpropitious, she looks upon the gentle as worthless. She avoids a hero like a thorn, leaps over a courteous man as if he were a snake, shuns the giver of charities as a nightmare. She keeps away from the temperate and mocks at the wise. Her ways are full of jugglery and contradiction. Though creating a fever she also produces a chill; though rising from water she increases thirst; though of earthly mould she is invisible; though attached to the highest, she really loves only the base. For the poisonous weeds of desire she is like a fostering shower; for the deer of the senses, she is like the hunter's alluring song; for the picture of virtue she is like a polluting cloud of smoke. Lakshmi is the cataract filming over the light of wisdom, the lair of the serpent of sin, the watchtower for the monster of pride, the prologue of the drama of deception. Under her influence the heart of a king becomes the abode of shameful thoughts.

And remember, my dear Chandrapida, that success is a very uncertain commodity. Sometimes kings are puffed up by their achievements, and their natures are poisoned as if by an accumulation of diseases. Moreover, kings are liable to be tortured by the senses which, though only five in number, turn into a thousand. Pierced by the arrows of Cupid, kings, already sunk in luxury, are struck down and writhe in their agony. To make things worse, they are deceived and misled by rogues who hang around them. These evil companions describe gambling as a relaxation, adultery as a sign of cleverness, drinking as a necessary pleasure, neglect of the family as freedom from bonds. To them contempt for a *guru's* words is a sign of originality, disregard of the gods is freedom, flattery is forethought, recklessness is enterprise and lack of discrimination is impartiality. Guided by such boon companions, and cheated by their sweet words, kings become conceited and blind. Though subject to all the limitations of ordinary mortals, they regard themselves as divine beings. They esteem their glance as a favour and their words as a glorious blessing to others.

Burdened by the pride of their imaginary greatness, they neglect the gods, slight their teachers, and make fun of the learned as fools wasting their opportunities of pleasure in useless labour. They accept a counsellor's skill only in deception and appoint as their family priests only those charlatans who indulge in magical rites and the like.

My son, you must beware of the fate that overtakes such kings. You must strive never to earn the scorn of your people or the reproaches of your friends. Do not let wolfish courtiers prey upon you, nor rogues mislead you, nor women delude you. I know that you are steadfast and have been trained for a life of virtue. Yet it was my duty to have warned you. Now go and enjoy your consecration to kinghood. Bear the yoke which will be handed over to you, as your forefathers have borne it. Bend the heads of your enemies and raise the heads of your friends. Crown yourself with glory.'

Having tendered this advice Shukanasa was silent. Chandrapida felt that these words had made him pure and radiant. He carefully pondered over them as he returned to his palace. Some days later King Tarapida chose an auspicious moment for anointing his son. A thousand chieftains gathered in a vast pavilion. The vessel of consecration was raised aloft. Holy water was brought from distant pools, rivers and seas. Tears of joy mingled with this water. Royal glory passed on to Chandrapida without leaving Tarapida, just as a creeper, still clasping its own tree, passes on to another tree. The prince was garlanded with fresh white flowers and adorned with a necklace of pearls. An amulet was placed on his right arm and he was clad in new robes of silk. After he had received the respectful homage of all the assembled kings, a mighty drum was sounded and the prince set out on his victorious course. The sound of that drum, struck by golden drumsticks, was like the sound of doomsday. It seemed as though the foundations of the earth were being shaken by an earthquake. The echo of that drum of victory spread through the three worlds and reached the peaks of the Himalayas. Chandrapida came down from the throne; and with him descended the glory of his rivals on earth. He left the hall of assembly and made ready to start on his wanderings.

The chieftains rose hastily and, as they collided with each other in confusion, the ground was strewn with their pearls as if grains of rice were being scattered as a good omen for the prince's journey. An elephant was brought, adorned with all the auspicious signs, and Patralekha was placed inside the howdah. The prince mounted. An umbrella was raised over him, white like the whirlpool of the milky ocean. As he started, he saw the horizon bathed in rich sunlight. It seemed as though the brilliance of his own majesty was lighting up the four quarters. Vaishampayana kept close to the prince and it seemed as if the moon and the sun had come together. When the two friends, accompanied by their numerous followers, advanced, it appeared that the earth was made of horses, the horizon of elephants, the atmosphere of parasols. The sky seemed to dissolve in dust. Gazing at this spectacle Vaishampayana said, 'Prince, is anything left unconquered by your mighty father? Is there a region of earth still unsubdued, a fortress not yet captured, treasures not yet acquired? Are there any continents not yet colonized, any kings not yet humbled? When 1 look at this army I recall accounts of the *Mahabharata*. It is a marvel that the earth has not split into a thousand pieces by the weight of this army, and that its muscles, the mountains, have not burst asunder.'

The prince, however, was dejected at the thought of his separation from his parents. Throughout the day he continued to travel and, when night came, he still thought of his parents and of Shukanasa. Vaishampayana rested on a couch near his own, and Patralekha slept on a blanket placed on the ground. The prince conversed with them, recalling memories of the time he had spent in his father's nouse. At dawn he got up and continued his advance. His army seemed to swell at every stage of the journey. It seemed to hollow out the earth, shake

the mountains, dry the rivers, batter down the fortresses and empty
the lakes. Chandrapida humbled the haughty, exalted the meek,
destroyed the wicked and protected the needy. He anointed tributary
princes, gathered treasures, accepted gifts and inscribed edicts. Thus
treading the earth from shore to shore, and turning the ocean's expanse
gray with the dust his army, he wandered for a long time. Within three
years he had subdued the limits of earthly space.

VI

In the course of his wanderings Chandrapida occupied Suvarnapura
and, as his men were weary, encamped there. One day, during his
sojourn in this prosperous city, the prince had a desire to go on a hunt.
He mounted Indrayudha and roamed through the woods. In an
obscure part of the forest he had a glimpse of a pair of *Kinnaras*. The
sight was strange to him. Eager to capture them, he gave rein to his
horse and pursued the unearthly beings. But the *Kinnaras* hurried away
and started climbing a steep hill. Again and again Chandrapida
approached them, but every time they eluded him. At last he was
checked by the steep ascent and stopped.

He discovered that he had strayed far from his companions and
did not know how to get back to Suvarnapura. The prince laughed at
his own folly and reflected: 'Why have I behaved like a child? Why
have I wearied myself for nothing? What would I have gained if I had
got *the Kinnaras?* Indeed, I have acted thoughtlessly. The good work
that I was doing has been interrupted. I have forsaken my friends and
earned for myself the ridicule of every one. And now who can show
me the way to the city! I am in a mighty forest at the foot of a high
mountain. It is well known that Suvarnapura is the northernmost city
on earth. So it is clear that this mountain must be Kailasa. I must now
go south and try to rejoin my companions.'

Thinking in this fashion, Chandrapida left Indrayudha in a grassland, and himself roamed about in search of water. After some time he came upon the wet footprints of wild elephants and inferred that water was near at hand. He followed the track which led him on the slopes of Kailasa. Climbing higher and higher he saw a clump of lofty trees, rising like a mighty cloud heavy with the weight of rain. The breeze, soft and dewy, seemed to woo him. It was cool, aromatic with the scent of flowers, and musical with the wafted melody of swans. He entered the grove and discovered a lake. It was the incomparable Lake Achchoda.

Never had he seen a lake so beautiful. It was like the mirror of Lakshmi, like the crystal chamber of the goddess of earth. It was like the Himalayas liquefied, like molten moonlight, like Siva's benign smile transformed into water. It seemed as if the merit of the three worlds had congealed in the shape of that lake, as if the mass of autumn clouds had been poured into some huge vessel. It was a lake that seemed to have been fashioned from the pure hearts of ascetics, from the virtues of good men, from the eyes of gazelles and the rays of pearls. Its expanse was vast; indeed it seemed to be endless, like a philosopher's futile argument.

At the sight of that lake Chandrapida's weariness left him. He reflected: 'Although my pursuit of the *Kinnaras* was fruitless, my eyes have been rewarded. I have seen the perfection of all that causes joy, the vanishing point of all that is worthy of sight. Now I understand why Siva never leaves the Kailasa mountain; surely it is because he cannot bear to be away from this lake.' As the prince was absorbed in these thoughts, Indrayudha, having eaten his fill of the delicious grass, rolled on the ground, and drank the cool water of the lake. When the horse was thoroughly refreshed, Chandrapida tied him with a golden chain to a tree nearby and himself came to the shore of the lake. He washed his hands and supped on pieces of lotus-fibre. Then, gathering some lotus leaves, he made a couch for himself on a rock shaded by creepers, folded his cloak to serve as a pillow, and lay down to sleep.

After he had rested for a little while, the prince was awakened by the distant sound of music. Indrayudha, too, pricked up his ears and arched his neck in the direction from which the sound came. The prince left his bed of lotus-leaves and looked this way and that, amazed that a human voice, mingled with the notes of a lute, should be heard in such a deserted place. The melody was so enchanting that he was impelled to advance towards the spot from where it seemed to originate. Followed by Indrayudha, and accompanied by fawns spellbound like himself, he reached a secluded grove in which there was a temple of Siva. As he passed through the door the pollen of blossoms from the overhanging creepers fell upon his head, and he was thus forced to appear before the God as if smeared with ash. Inside the shrine he beheld the emblem of Siva, adorned with freshly plucked lotus-buds. And right in front of the deity he saw a maiden singing a hymn.

The splendour of her beauty seemed to turn the entire temple into ivory. Her face shone as though it were a storehouse of penance gathered for many years. Her complexion was so fair that she seemed to be encased in crystal, or soaked in a sea of milk. She was like the brightness of Siva's smile, like the moonlight which zealously tries to overcome the darkness of Siva's neck. In her purity she was like the three Vedas, or like the germ of a golden age. She seemed to have been fashioned from the whiteness of swans, or to have emerged from the moon's orb, or to have been manufactured out of ivory flakes. Her locks fell luxuriantly upon her shoulders. Her brow was smeared with ash, pure as the dust of stars ground by the hoofs of the sun's heavenly steeds. She seemed to be a maiden of eighteen years, but her age could not be counted by earthly reckoning since she was like a goddess.

As Chandrapida bowed before the blessed Siva he reflected: 'Each wonder seems to be followed by a greater one. When I was chasing the *Kinnaras*, I reached a spot of incredible beauty. In my search for water I stumbled upon a wondrous lake. And now, seeking the source of a melody, I see this divine maiden.' Meanwhile the maiden had finished her song. Her lute was silent. It appeared as if a lotus pool had suddenly become still through the departure of humming bees. The maiden got up, made obeisance to Siva, and then looked at Chandrapida. Her glance was so pure that the prince felt as though she were sprinkling holiness upon him by her eyes. In a gentle voice she hailed him as a guest and invited him to visit her home so that the duties of hospitality might be performed.

At a distance of hundred paces from the temple he saw the cave in which she lived. It was moist with the spray of mountain torrents and veiled by the dense foliage of *tamala* trees. Inside the cave a number of pitchers stood in a corner. There was a bed of bark with a gourd by its side. In another corner a pair of sandals made of coconut matting were suspended on a peg. Pressed by her, Chandrapida accepted her hospitality and drank the cool water offered to him in a leafy cup. She requested him to relate his adventures, and Chandrapida described how he had strayed to the foot of Kailasa while pursuing a pair of *Kinnaras*. After a while the maiden rose and walked about under the trees with a bowl in her hand. To Chandrapida's amazement the trees cast down their fruits of their own accord. When enough was gathered she returned to the cave with him and the two enjoyed their repast.

Emboldened by her kindness Chandrapida said, 'Noble lady, I am bewildered. My curiosity has got the better of my diffidence and I must request you to tell me about yourself. Which is the race honoured by your birth? Why have you, tender as a blossom, imposed upon yourself the life of an ascetic? Why are you dwelling alone in this deserted forest? And how is it that your body, though formed out of the five elements, has attained such heavenly brilliance?' The maiden listened to his enquiry in silence and then, as she tried to answer him, her eyes welled up and a stream of tears flooded her cheeks. Those pearly tears were saturated with the purity of her mind. They were like the distilled essence of renunciation dropping from her bright eyes. She wept noiselessly for some time and then, bathing her eyes with water and drying her face with the end of her robe, she narrated the story of her life.

And this is what Chandrapida heard from her.

VII

Oh Prince, why do you want to hear the unhappy story of my ascetic life? My heart has been a tyrant to me and my destiny has been a hard one. However, since you are so eager to hear it, I must narrate my tale of sorrow. Perhaps you know that in the abode of gods there are maidens known as *Apsarases*. There are many families of these maidens. Some are sprung from the mind of Brahma, others from the Vedas, and still others from moonbeams. In one such family of *Apsarases* once a maiden was born named Gauri. She was so fair that she seemed to have been made out of the digits of the moon poured into a single stream. When she grew up she was courted by Hamsa, the king of the *Gandharvas*. They were united as the lotus pool is united with the autumn. She became the Queen of the *Gandharvas* and enjoyed every happiness in company with her husband. To this pair I was born an only daughter. My father celebrated my birth with great festivities and gave me the name of Mahashweta. In his palace I spent my childhood. *Gandharva* maidens fondly passed me from lap to lap and I grew in the cool shade of their affection. In the course of time youth came to me as bees come to the flowers and honey to the bees.

One day I went with my mother to bathe in the lake which you have already seen. It was the season of spring and all the lotuses were in bloom. I worshipped the images of Siva carved on the rocks by Parvati herself countless ages ago. The bowers were covered by creepers whose blossoms were weighed down by bees. The mangoes were flowering; honey oozed out of the holes in their buds pierced by the cuckoos. The serpents, frightened by the murmur of white peacocks, had deserted the sandal avenues. Lost in the charms of this wooded spot I wandered for a long time. Suddenly the fragrance of a flower, borne on the wind reached me. It was a scent that drowned the fragrance of all other flowers, although the entire forest was in blossom. It anointed all my senses and overwhelmed my perception. Swarms of bees followed it, seeking to make it their very own. It was a perfume fit for the gods.

Looking for the source of this heavenly fragrance, I came upon a youthful ascetic on his way to the lake. Such was his splendour that he seemed to be enclosed in a cage of quivering lightning. His eyebrows were like arches rising high above the abode of human perfection. His nose was sharp and aquiline, his eyes were gentle like a deer's, his lips rosy with the glow of youth. The thread on his shoulder was like the bent string of Cupid's bow. He carried a dainty pitcher in one hand and a rosary in the other. He was clad in the bark of a heavenly coral tree, bright like the eyelids of a dove. And he was accompanied by another youthful ascetic, his equal in age, a companion in every way worthy of himself.

Looking up at the ascetic's face I saw a bunch of flowers placed on one of his ears. Now I understood where the overpowering perfume had come from. But I forgot the fragrance as soon as I looked upon the beauty of the ascetic's face. I had thus far imagined that the Creator had compounded all the beauty of his Universe in Cupid. Now I found another surpassing Cupid himself. When Brahma made the moon to gladden the earth, when he made the heavenly lotus as Lakshmi's palace of joy, he was only practising to acquire the necessary skill for the creation of this ascetic's face.

Suddenly Love, the comrade of beauty, enthralled me—Love who does not care for good or ill and who is always ready to assail young hearts. I was captivated as the intoxicating spring captivates bees. With my eyelashes half closed I looked upon him and drank him in. I wanted to offer him my heart and to enter into him with my entire soul. I knew it was a feeling unworthy of a noble maiden, but I could not master myself. A storm of sighs swept from me. How cruel was Cupid, to have kindled in me ideas of love towards a cold ascetic! I thought that he must be scorning me in his heart. With a supreme effort I restrained myself and was about to leave the place when I remembered that a holy man has to be revered, whatever the circumstances. So I bent down before him, my garland swaying on my wavy hair and my earrings brushing my shoulders. To my surprise I found that he was also thrilled by my sight. He wavered like a flower in the wind. The rosary in his hand trembled, as if afraid that he might break his sacred vows. His pupils were dilated and his glances turned the atmosphere into a lotus grove. When I saw his condition my love was redoubled. I advanced and asked his friend, 'Sir, what is the name of His Reverence? And from what tree were these flowers collected? Their scent is unique and has kindled my curiosity.'

The companion replied, 'Surely you have heard of Shwetaketu, the great sage. Once, gathering lotuses for the worship of gods, he went down to the heavenly Ganga. Lakshmi, enthroned on a white lotus close by, saw him and was struck by the arrows of love. Shwetaketu, in his turn, was won over by the very first glance of Lakshmi. A son was born and was given the name of Pundarika. My friend, whom you see adorned with these fragrant flowers, is none other than Pundarika. As for the flowers that have excited your curiosity, they come from the Parijata tree which emerged when the ocean of milk was churned by gods and titans. It was given to my friend as a gift by a nymph.'

While his friend was speaking, Pundarika himself approached me and said, 'Why do you bother to ask all this? If the flowers please you, they are yours. Take them.' And gently taking the flowers from his ears he placed them on mine. As his fingers brushed against my cheeks he dropped his rosary. But before it reached the ground I seized it and placed it on my neck. Within a few moments our hearts had understood each other.

I was startled by the voice of my umbrella-bearer who reminded me that my mother had finished her bath and it was time to go home. Like a newly captured elephant, rebellious at the first touch of the hook, my mind was being reluctantly dragged away. Meanwhile Pundarika's friend was upbraiding him for his lack of self-control. 'Where is your firmness?' he said. 'And what has happened to your holy vows? If even men like you are swept off their feet like this, all knowledge will become worthless and the teachings of the *gurus* will lose their meaning. Even your rosary is being carried off by this worthless girl.'

Pundarika said sheepishly, 'Do not misunderstand me, dear Kapinjala. I shall certainly not allow this maiden to take my rosary with her.' And then, feigning wrath, he turned to me and said, 'What kind of sport is this, maiden? I shall not let you go until you return my rosary.' At this I loosened a string of pearls from my neck, placed it in his outstretched hand, and took leave of him. I do not know how I managed to join my companions and reach home. I was like a river driven backwards.

Entering my chamber, I dismissed all my attendants and stood alone with my face pressed against the jewelled window. Ignorant of the course of love, I did not know which way to turn and what remedy to seek. I gazed into empty space, thinking of Pundarika. I longed to ask the breeze where my beloved was going. I foolishly tried to get news of him from the scent of flowers and the songs of birds. Though he was far away I turned towards him as the lotus turns to the sun, the waves of the ocean to the moon, or the peacock to the cloud. I fondly placed his rosary on my neck and recalled the delicate touch of his fingers.

After some time my companion, Taralika, came to me and said, 'Princess, one of those ascetics followed me and asked about you. When I told him your name and ancestry, he said: 'Dear lady, young as you are I nevertheless see in you great steadfastness. Please help me. Carry a letter from me to Princess Mahashweta.' When I promised to do his bidding, he plucked a young shoot from a tree nearby, crushed it on a stone, and tearing a piece from his bark garment wrote these words with his nail.'

I snatched the letter from Taralika's hand. This is how it read: 'As a swan in a Himalayan lake is lured by the treacherous arms of a creeper on the bank, so is my heart beguiled by your pearl necklace.' When I read this message my lovesick mind, already distraught, lost its bearings altogether. The letter did to me what a dark night does to a shortsighted man, a conjurer's trick to a simpleton, atheistic philosophy to one already wavering. I spoke to my maid with great reverence. I cajoled and flattered her into talking about him. I asked a thousand questions about Pundarika's companion and, bolting the doors of my room, heard Taralika's answers again and again.

The sun, like a ball suspended in the sky, became crimson. The lotuses closed their eyes, as though swooning at the sun's departure. Before the night was far advanced, an attendant approached me and said, 'Princess, one of the two hermits whom you met has come here. He says you have in your possession a string of beads, and he begs of you to return it.' The very mention of a hermit made my heart pound and my breath came heavily as I asked the attendant to admit the visitor. A few moments later I saw Kapinjala, who is to Pundarika what youth is to beauty, love to youth, spring to love, and the breeze to spring. I brought a seat for him and, when he was reluctanly compelled to accept it, I washed his feet. He looked at Taralika and his glance suggested that he wanted to speak to me privately. I told him that I had no secrets from my friend and that he could speak freely.

Kapinjala exclaimed, 'Alas, what can I say? Through shame I can hardly utter the words that I have framed in my mind. My dearest friend, once a passionless ascetic firm as a rock, has become a pitiable object of Cupid's sport. You will recall, noble princess, that I rebuked Pundarika for his behaviour, so unworthy of a holy man. I left him in considerable anger. When I calmed down, I returned to the spot where I had last seen him. He was not there. I knew that love had deprived him of his judgment, and I felt anxious about his welfare. I wandered for hours, searching every bower, glade and avenue. At last I discovered him in a thicket of creepers on the bank of a lake. He was like one in a trance, or like one suddenly struck down by paralysis. Tears silently trickled down his eyes. His suffering was unbearable. Even the creepers that shaded him trembled and sighed as they watched him. Trees dropped upon his head the pollen of their fresh blossoms as a powder to subdue the fever of love. Pundarika was draped in paleness, like the new moon; he had dwindled, like a river in May; he was fading away, like a sandal tree whose roots suddenly become diseased.

With great effort he opened his eyes and looked at me languidly. His deep sighs were punctuated by indistinct words that I could not make out. When he seemed a little more steady I again exhorted him to control himself. I told him that an ascetic who listens to love, waters a poison tree and mistakes a burning piece of coal for a jewel. He leaned on me and said: 'Kapinjala, you are lucky. Cupid has spared you the torments that I endure. To me all talk of stability, reflection or judgment has become meaningless. The hour for good advice has gone by. You see my wretched plight. My heart is seething, my eyes dissolve and my entire being is on fire. Do what my condition demands. Please understand that it is no use speaking of good and evil.' It was clear to me that Pundarika had gone too far to be turned back. So I made an effort to preserve his life.

I collected some tender lotus-fibres from the lake and prepared a couch for him. As he rested there I anointed him from head to foot with the juice of soft sandal twigs. I soothed his brow with camphor-dust and fanned him with a plantain leaf. It was painful for me to reflect that so promising an ascetic had become a victim of that miscreant, Love. But I consoled myself with the thought that Love is a tyrant who may strike any one, high or low. Nor are his depredations confined to the human race. The lotus falls in love with the sun, lightning clings to the cloud. Then why blame Pundarika who had, after all, a human heart?

Noble lady, I have described Pundarika's condition. As a friend my one duty now is to save his life. The fever of love admits no delay. It is now for you to. judge what is to be done.'

When Kapinjala stopped speaking, I hardly knew what to say to him. The certainty that my love was reciprocated made me supremely happy. I never doubted, even for a moment, that Kapinjala had narrated only the truth. It was inconceivable that there should be any trace of exaggeration in the words of so balanced and restrained a person. I had hardly recovered from my confusion when a messenger entered announcing that my mother, the queen, was visiting me. Kapinjala hastily took his leave, with a last appealing glance at me. My mother came and stayed with me for a long time, but my mind was far away and I did not hear a word of what she said. At last she left me and returned to her chamber.

It was the hour of sunset. The west was crimson, the lotus pools were turning green, the east was a mass of deep blue and the entire world was gradually overcome by blackness. I took counsel with Taralika about the predicament in which I found myself. By transgressing the code of conduct dictated by my birth and position, I would bring disgrace to my parents. On the other hand, by courting death I might break the heart of Pundarika, and that might drive Kapinjala to despair. As the night advanced, my suffering became unendurable. Already consumed by fever, I seemed to be subjected to a shower of white-hot coals. Taralika asked me not to think of the rules of conduct, or the prestige of my parents, at such a moment. She said, 'Your love is like an ocean whose manifold waves are swelling at moonrise. Let me fetch Pundarika here. There is no other way.'

But I decided to go to him myself. From Kapinjala's account it was obvious that Pundarika was in no condition to move about. By and by the firmament was flooded with moonlight. The sky became a sandy island in the river of night. Accompanied by Taralika I set out. Pundarika's rosary was on my neck and the bunch of Parijata flowers given by him adorned one of my ears. Dressed in red silk that seemed to have been woven from the rays of rubies, I slipped out of the palace. The strong scent of Parijata flowers attracted a swarm of bees which seemed to form a blue veil around me. The moon, stretching out its rays, seemed to urge me on with its long fingers.

As I approached, my right eye quivered. My heart seemed to sink with anxiety at this ill-omen. My fears were soon realized. I heard Kapinjala bewailing and sobbing. 'Alas, everything is lost!' he cried, 'I am undone. Cupid, cruel demon that you are, what evil deed have you compassed! Oh wicked, wanton Mahashweta, in what way had my poor friend harmed you? Why have you led him to destruction? Venerable Shwetaketu, do you know that your very life is stolen from you? Dharma, you are now helpless—your protector is gone. Knowledge, you are widowed. Alas, where shall I seek refuge? My friend, what has happened to your love for me? Why have you deserted me?'

As I heard Kapinjala utter these pathetic words, my own life seemed to be ebbing away. I advanced on the rough ground as quickly as my condition permitted. I stumbled at every step and my cloak was torn as I passed through tangled creepers. At last I saw Pundarika on a couch of lotus leaves. He lay absolutely still, as though listening to the sound of my steps. The garland of lotus fibres on his neck bound him, as if with a chain of moonbeams, to drag him forcibly to another world. Before my very eyes he yielded up his life.

I do not know how long and in what way I lamented the cruel departure of Pundarika. But I do recall that I suddenly asked Taralika to gather dry wood and make a pile for me. As I was preparing to join the lord of my life in the other world, a strange being left the moon's pale orb and descended upon the earth. He was wearing a silken vesture, white as foam, which waved in the breeze. His face was bright with the rays that shot from the gems in his ears. His necklace, made of large pearls, looked like a cluster of stars. Lofty in stature, with all the marks of greatness, he seemed to purify the space through which he moved. This heavenly being gently picked up Pundarika and said to me, in a voice as deep as it was sonorous, 'Mahashweta, you must not think of taking your own life. You will be united with him again.' And with these words he soared into the sky, carrying Pundarika with him. Before I realized what had happened Kapinjala followed the heavenly being and pursued him in the sky, crying: 'Where are you taking my friend, you monster!'

Kapinjala's disappearance was for me a second bereavement. My grief was redoubled and I was overcome by a feeling of utter helplessness. Taralika shook me out of my stupor. 'What a miracle!' she said. 'Such godlike beings never make deceptive statements. Princess, you must take courage. I am sure Kapinjala will return and tell us what has befallen Pundarika. You must preserve your life and bear your grief. Your reunion with him is certain.'

These words raised in me the illusion that my life was worth prolonging. I spent that night on the bank of the lake. To me, in my fathomless misery, it was like a night of doom extending over a thousand years. I tossed on the ground, my face smothered by my dishevelled locks. At dawn I got up, bathed in the lake, and resolved not to inflict death upon myself. I picked up all the things that Pundarika had used—his pitcher, his garments and his rosary. And then, taking the vow of asceticism, I came to the temple of Siva. Next day my parents came and tried to persuade me to return home. They prayed and admonished, with many tender words and streams of tears. But I stuck to my determination. Since then I have been living here. I sustain my body on water and on the fruits and tubers that grow wild in this region. Such is my life—cold, fruitless and without joy.

VIII

Mahashweta had now come to the end of her story. She covered her face with the edge of her bark garment, and it appeared as though the moon was obscured by an autumn cloud. Unable to suppress her pent-up emotions she gave way to renewed weeping. A torrent of tears gushed from her eyes and her breath was choked with sobs.

Chandrapida was filled with admiration as much for her modesty and austerity as for her divine beauty. He looked upon her serene and pure countenance and said in a gentle voice, 'Only those should weep who are afraid of pain, or are devoid of gratitude. Such people can do very little that is worthy of love and can only show their feelings through idle tears. But you have left nothing undone that love may demand. You have despised earthly pleasures. You have relinquished the joys of power and wealth. Your delicate body has been subjected to stern penance. Above all, you have made a supreme effort to prolong your life. It is easy to abdicate from life under the weight of unbearable sorrow. But it needs heroism to carry the burden of grief. Therefore, noble Mahashweta, please restrain your tears. Your companion, Taralika, was right when she said that the words of heavenly beings are not uttered lightly. You have been promised reunion with Pundarika and I am sure the promise will be kept.'

As Chandrapida was consoling her in this way the sun was about to sink, as if overwhelmed with grief at Mahashweta's story. Gradually the horizon was suffused with the glow of sunset, soft like a piece of silk dyed in the juice of lotuses. The breeze, cooled by the dew, wandered at leisure on its aerial track marked by the fragrance of wild flowers. The earth was soon enveloped in darkness. Birds fell asleep one by one. Mahashweta repeated her evening prayers, washed her feet, and lay down on her humble couch of bark. Chandrapida, too, made for himself a bed of branches on the other rock in the cave and retired. He pondered for some time over the strange story that he had heard. Then he asked, 'Where is your friend, Taralika? Did she not come with you when you left your home?' Mahashweta replied, 'Sir, Taralika has gone to the kingdom of the *Gandharvas*, carrying a message for my dearest friend, Kadambari.'

Chandrapida was curious to know about Kadambari, a name that had not been mentioned by Mahashweta in the course of her long narrative. So he said, 'Now that we have conversed so freely with each other, and you have shared your sorrow with me, I shall be grateful if you tell me about Kadambari also.'

Mahashweta said, 'Kadambari is the daughter of Chitraratha, King of the *Gandharvas*, and his queen, Madira. Even in her childhood she was regarded as exceptionally pretty; now, in the bloom of youth, she is a paragon of loveliness, unmatched in heaven or earth. Moreover, she is as generous and affectionate as she is beautiful. We have been

friends since we were little children. We have played together in the
dust; and together we have learnt to dance and sing. When she heard
of my love for Pundarika, so cruelly thwarted by death, she made a
resolve not to accept a husband while I was enduring my grief in
loneliness. She declared that if her parents tried to marry her off against
her will she would end her life by fasting or poison. King Chitraratha
and Queen Madira are sunk in deep dejection. Only this morning I
received a despatch from them, imploring me to dissuade Kadambari
from her stern purpose. That is why I have sent Taralika with the
message that if Kadambari is anxious to see me alive she must not bring
sorrow to her parents and must do what they desire.'

Early next morning, when Mahashweta and Chandrapida had just
finished their prayers, Taralika returned to the cave. She was
accompanied by a *Gandharva* boy named Keyuraka. Both of them were
surprised to see a stranger in their midst. Chandrapida's wonderful
personality made a deep impression upon them and they respectfully
bowed to him before taking their seats.

Mahashweta made eager enquiries about her friend. Taralika said,
'Princess Kadambari is well. But her reply to your message is such that
I do not have the heart to repeat it. This *Gandharva* boy will convey
it to you.' Mahashweta anxiously looked at Keyuraka, who delivered
this message from Kadambari: 'Why has Taralika been sent? To test
my feelings? Or is this a subtle method of blaming me for staying on
at home while Mahashweta is spending her days in that desolate place?
Or has Mahashweta wearied of my friendship? Or is she angry with
me for some mysterious reason? I cannot understand how she can
expect me to heed her advice. I shall never hearken to the call of Love,
that pitiless tyrant, while my dearest friend sorrows for Pundarika night
and day, avoiding the very sight of humankind. No one can shake me
from this resolve.'

Mahashweta was disappointed. She pondered over the situation for a long time and then dismissed Keyuraka who returned to Hemakuta, the capital of the *Gandharvas*. Then, turning to Chandrapida, Mahashweta said, 'Prince, why don't you come with me to the kingdom of the *Gandharvas*? You will see many wonders and gather novel experiences in that strange and beautiful land. I shall introduce you to that treasure of loveliness, Kadambari, who is like my second self. Perhaps you may be able to remove this whim from her mind. You have been kind to me. Your sympathy has lightened my grief. Now please crown our friendship by acceding to my request.'

Chandrapida readily agreed to this suggestion and together they travelled to the land of the *Gandharvas*. Reaching Hemakuta, the capital city, they passed through golden arches and, crossing a number of courts and pavilions, approached the women's apartments in the palace. At the sight of Mahashweta every one rejoiced and messengers ran this way and that to spread the news of her arrival. Chandrapida marvelled at all the curiosities that he saw there. It seemed to be a world of women, a continent immersed in the waves of feminine charms, a race created by Prajapati out of dislike for men. Here all was Beauty and Love. Cupid was the supreme deity.

Tanks were being scented with perfumed powders; jewelled lamps were being arranged in dark avenues; ripe pomegranates were being covered with pearly nets to keep off the birds; emerald-green arbours were being swept with golden brooms; the swans were being fed on lotus honey; the tame peacocks were being taken to their luxurious shower-baths. The pigeons were enjoying their meal of mango-buds. Maidens were weaving garlands. Singing lessons were going on in apartments specially furnished and equipped with the finest instruments. The caged parrots and *mainas* were receiving their lessons.

At last Chandrapida saw Princess Kadambari herself in the middle of a spacious pavilion. She rested on her bent arms, leaning on a white pillow. Her couch was covered with blue silk. Attendants were fanning her with peacock tails. By her side sat Keyuraka, whom Chandrapida had already met. He was describing Chandrapida's beauty and grace, while the princess listened with great interest.

As soon as he saw Kadambari, the prince's heart became agitated like ocean-waves at high tide. He reflected: 'What noble deeds have my eyes performed that they are permitted to feast on such beauty? Surely the Creator must have fashioned her out of digits gathered from everything in the Universe that is beautiful. He must have spent so much energy in moulding her that tears of fatigue must have fallen from his eyes, giving rise to all the lotuses in the world.' And as he was plunged in these reflections his eyes met hers. Confused by the sight of Kadambari, yet illumined by her gaze, he stood for a moment as though rooted to the ground. Kadambari, too, was overwhelmed by Chandrapida's charm. As she rose from her seat, her jewels clashed and her silken robes fluttered through her heavy breathing. Her hand sought her heart, as if in an effort to touch Chandrapida's image that had entered in it.

Meanwhile Mahashweta had approached and Kadambari affectionately embraced her. Mahashweta introduced her to Chandrapida. 'Dear Kadambari,' she said, 'in the land of Bharata there is a mighty king named Tarapida who has impressed his seal on the four oceans. This is his son Chandrapida, who has instinctively become my friend. It is rarely that we meet a person of such exceptional intellect, and blessed with such power and glory, who is so easily swayed by friendship. I have brought him here so that you may see this specimen of Brahma's workmanship. Please do not stand on ceremony with him. Do not treat him as a stranger. Look upon him as your friend.' While Mahashweta was speaking, Kadambari looked at the prince sideways and her eyes were filled with tears of love. Her smile pervaded the atmosphere like a cloud of dust raised by her heart which had so hastily set out. Her delicate hand crept to her half-parted lips.

Mahashweta caressed her friend tenderly. She softly stroked her curly locks and touched the flowers with which she had adorned her ears. After a while an attendant approached with a gem-studded betel-box. Mahashweta asked Kadambari to honour the guest by offering him betel with her own hand. After great hesitation, and with a trembling hand, Kadambari managed to overcome her coyness and plucked up courage to offer betel leaves to Chandrapida. Her eyes rested on Mahashweta all the time, though her heart, if it had eyes, would have gazed upon Chandrapida. The murmur of her bracelets seemed to say: 'I am yours. Take me for your slave.'

A herald came and announced that Kadambari's parents were eager to meet Mahashweta. Before leaving the pavilion, Mahashweta suggested that the prince should be lodged in the House of Jewels on a hillock in the royal garden. Chandrapida went to the place allotted to him, followed by a number of serving-maids whom Kadambari selected to look after his comforts. He was guided by his old acquaintance, Keyuraka, and was soon installed in the House of Jewels.

IX

When he was gone, Kadambari sought the privacy of her own room and tried to master her agitation. As she thought of her conduct in the presence of Chandrapida, she was filled with shame. Modesty reproached her, self-respect rebuked her, youth warned of the pitfalls that awaited her. Nobility censured her, propriety chided her for being so easily swept off her feet by a stranger's charms. She blamed herself for forgetting Mahashweta's sorrow, for compromising her parents through her frivolous behaviour, and for overlooking her own vow not to hearken to the call of love. She reflected: 'What can I do? How can I ever undo this error? I made a promise to share Mahashweta's grief. My resolve was announced before all my friends and every one in the land of *Gandharvas* knows about it. Now, when gossip about my infatuation spreads, I shall become a laughingstock.' With these thoughts she decided to banish Chandrapida from her mind.

But the image of Chandrapida mocked at her resolve. It seemed to say: 'To banish me is for you a farewell to life.' She was bewildered. Her eyes saw nothing, but her memory saw everything. Her hand did not hold a brush, but her fancy painted the picture of her beloved. She collapsed, and arose, and collapsed again. After a while she got up from her couch, moved up to the window as if in a trance, and stood gazing at the hillock on which Chanarapida was staying.

Chandrapida, in his turn, was equally agitated. He wondered what right he had to hope that he would so quickly earn the love of Kadambari. It appeared to him that Cupid was dangling a conjurer's wand to beguile and charm him. He tried to divert himself by conversing with the attendants sent by Kadambari, and by listening to music and poetic recitation. But nothing helped to soothe him. After a short while he went out to see the park and climbed to the top of the hill. Kadambari saw him and, under the pretext of watching for Mahashweta's return, she ascended to the terrace. There she sat looking at the hill, while her maids held a golden umbrella above her head. She leaned for support on her dearest companions, Tamalika and Madalekha. When Mahashweta returned she had to leave the terrace and go down. Without any enthusiasm she went through the routine of bath, prayer and other duties.

Chandrapida stayed on at the top of the hill. Even his food was carried there. He sat on a slab of emerald which commanded a beautiful view of the green valley. By and by the day came to a close. The moon ascended with all the grace and majesty appropriate to the King of Heavenly Bodies. After a while, however, Chandrapida suddenly felt that the moon had become pale, and the moonlight had lost its brightness. He was baffled by this phenomenon for some time but

when he looked in the direction of Kadambari he understood that her
pearl necklace had eclipsed the moonlight. The princess was
approaching the hill along with her companions. Chandrapida advanced
to meet them. Kadambari stayed behind while Madalekha met the
prince halfway and accompanied him to the emerald seat. She said,
'Noble Prince, you have conquered the hearts of all of us. We have
nothing left and so we cannot offer you any suitable gift. Kadambari
has sent for you this necklace which emerged from the ocean when
the Lord churned the primeval waters. The Creator himself gave it to
Varuna, and Varuna passed it on to the king of the *Gandharvas.* The
King bestowed it on Kadambari, who is dearer to him than his own
life. It is a rare jewel. The like of it is not to be seen on heaven or
earth.'

Chandrapida accepted the gift with pleasure and gratitude.
Kadambari went back to her apartment. Having seen Chandrapida from
a distance, her longing to be with him became all the more unbearable.
The moon mounted higher and higher. It was like Cupid's royal
umbrella, like the ivory necklace of Night. Kadambari watched from
her window as the prince rested on a pearl-white slab at the edge of a
lotus-pool. Near the slab a pair of swans dozed blissfully, while
chakravaka birds sang a dirge of separation. Unable to endure her
parting from Chandrapida any longer, Kadambari sent Keyuraka to tell
him that she was coming to visit him.

The prince rose hastily and saw Kadambari who had come
without her royal insignia. She wore a single necklace. A single lotus
petal decked her ear. In her simplicity she stood like the very goddess
of moonrise. Approaching the slab she sat down on the ground.
Chandrapida, too, sat on the ground beside her; though Madalekha
entreated him to resume his seat. Kadambari made enquires about King
Tarapida and Queen Vilasavati. She expressed her curiosity about the
world of mortals, and especially about Ujjayini. All her questions were

whispered to Madalekha, who put them to the prince. This indirect conversation continued for some time and then Kadambari retired.

Next day Chandrapida paid a return visit. He found Kadambari in a bower where, along with Mahashweta, she was entertaining a company of wandering ascetic women. Hymns were chanted and portions from the *Mahabharata* were recited. When the ascetics left, Chandrapida looked at Mahashweta in such a way that she understood the silent appeal in his eyes. She turned to Kadambari and said, 'Dearest Kadambari, Chandrapida now wants to return. His companions must be in distress. But wherever he might go, his deep love will bind him to you forever. Like the sun and the day-lotus, like the moon and the lily of the night, you will always be together. So please give him leave for the time being.' The prince left Hemakuta with a heavy heart, carrying the image of Kadambari in his soul. His mind was wholly imbued with memories of the brief time he had spent in her company. She seemed to emerge mysteriously, trying to bar his way.

At last, weighed down by the cruel suffering of separation, he reached Mahashweta's hermitage. There he met his companions, who had discovered the hermitage by following the track left by Indrayudha. Chandrapida spent the day narrating his adventures to Vaishampayana and Patralekha. Early next morning he was surprised to see Keyuraka approaching him again. The prince made anxious enquiries about the welfare of Kadambari and Mahashweta. Keyuraka delivered a folded lotus-leaf, sealed by tender lotus-filaments set in sandal-paste. Opening the leaf. Chandrapida discovered beautiful gifts sent by Mahashweta along with a letter. Mahashweta had written: 'Happy are those from whose eyes your form is never absent. Your virtues, cool like moonlight when you are present, burn us like the rays of the sun when you are away. Without you the royal city of the *Gandharvas* is languid and lifeless. You know that I am an ascetic and have renounced everything. And yet my heart longs to see you again.

You can imagine what Kadambari is going through. Think of her, and save her by returning to Hemakuta. I am sending the necklace which Kadambari had presented to you and which you left behind on your couch.'

Having read this letter Chandrapida felt exceedingly sad. He wore the necklace sent by Mahashweta and asked Keyuraka about Kadambari's condition. Keyuraka said, 'Noble Prince, how shall I describe what the Princess is enduring? When you left Hemakuta, she climbed to the terrace and gazed at the House of Jewels where you had spent the night. After a while she descended and went to the park. She climbed the hill and longingly looked at every object with which you had come in contact. She touched the rock on which your hand had rested, the tank by the side of which you had listened to the song of birds, the stream in which you had dipped your fingers before worshipping Siva, the crystal stone on which your food had been served and the pearly slab which still bore marks of the sandal juice with which your hands were scented. Overcome by emotion, she hurried back to her room and threw herself upon her bed. She was racked by the pain that had entered every fibre, muscle and joint of her body. She passed the night open-eyed with bitter grief. And at dawn she summoned me. As soon as she saw me, she despatched me here to get news of you.'

Chandrapida could not tarry a moment longer. Indrayudha was hastily saddled, Vaishampayana was placed in charge of the camp, and the prince once more started for Hemakuta accompanied by Patralekha. His eagerness, no less than his familiarity with the path, lent speed to his progress. Very soon his eyes rejoiced as the dim outlines of Kadambari's palace emerged upon the horizon.

Mahashweta was the first to greet him. He bowed to her respectfully and then saluted Kadambari. Keyuraka presented Patralekha to the princess, extolling her qualities and describing her as 'Prince Chandrapida's most favoured friend'. Kadambari thought: 'How partial is Prajapati to women of the earth! They have the fortune to bask in the presence of a man like Chandrapida. *Apsarases* and *Kinnaris* have no such luck!'

Chandrapida was now at the height of his happiness. He divided his time between Hemakuta and his own camp below the hermitage of Mahashweta. Patralekha and Kadambari had become such close friends that Chandrapida had to agree to leave Patralekha at Hemakuta. Vaishampayana was, of course, with him in the camp. One day a messenger from Ujjayini arrived. Chandrapida made anxious enquiries about the welfare of his parents. The messenger produced a letter and the prince opened it with trembling hands.

The letter was from King Tarapida. After assuring his son that there was no cause for anxiety, and that everyone was well, the king had written: 'But, dearest Chandrapida, why have you been away for such a long time? Our hearts long for the sight of your sweet face. The queen pines for you. Shukanasa also is eagerly waiting for you and Vaishampayana. Enough of your conquests. Return to Ujjayini at once.' Chandrapida left Vaishampayana in charge of the camp, instructed that one of the senior officers should escort Patralekha back to Ujjayini, and himself made preparations to return. When everything was ready, he saddled Indrayudha and turned towards his native land.

His heart was weighed down by uneasiness. He reflected: 'What will Kadambari think of me? I am proving myself unworthy of her love. I promised to be near her, and now the call of my parents compels me to leave so suddenly. 'My body is moving towards Ujjayini, but my heart will remain at Hemakuta. I have written a bond of slavery to Kadambari for a thousand births. The entire land of *Gandharvas* will look upon me as a deserter and Mahashweta—how will she interpret my sudden departure? She brought me and Kadambari together in the hope that her dearest friend would gain happiness and now I am shattering her dream.'

Such were his thoughts as he slowly descended the slopes of Kailasa, leaving the world of *Gandharvas* behind him.

X

A few days later Patralekha joined him, and he felt that she had become dearer to him than ever before; for had she not lived with Kadambari, who was the very breath of his life? Chandrapida was eager to get all the news from Hemakuta. Through sheer impatience he drove away a pair of swans sleeping peacefully in a leafy bower. Reclining on a bed of fresh hibiscus blossoms, he asked Patralekha to tell him about Kadambari's condition.

Patralekha said, 'My Lord, on the day you left Hemakuta the princess did not let me out of her sight for a single moment. She spoke little, but gazed into my eyes and pressed my hand tenderly. The next morning she left the winter palace and ascended to the summer house, leaning upon me for support. She dismissed all her attendants, and pushed aside the tame geese that had followed us. When a peacock persisted in demanding her attention, she gave him a piece of betel broken by her own teeth, as though it were a bribe to keep him quiet.

For a while she remained in that bower like a mysterious wood-goddess. At last, recovering her speech with great effort, she said, 'Dearest Patralekha, to whom shall I confide my suffering, if not to you? I am ashamed of my unmaidenly levity. I have brought odium upon our race, pure as moonbeams. Without my parents' approval, without the blessings of my elders, without any exchange of gifts or pictures, I have formed an attachment with a stranger. Ever since I met Chandrapida, may heart, tender as a lotus filament, is crushed into pulp. Why has he treated me lightly? Does such conduct befit a prince of noble descent? His love has consumed first my reserve and then my heart. Only by death can I cleanse myself Farewell, dearest friend, until we meet in another birth.'

'Do not speak in this way, Princess,' I said. 'What offence has Chandrapida committed? In what way has he been unfair to you?'

Kadambari said, 'Ah, that cunning villain comes to me in my dreams. He bewilders my mind with vain desires. He sends me messages filled with mad hopes and embraces me in secluded corners of the forest. The flatterer dries my wet cheeks with his cool breath and draws me to himself. He brooks no refusal. When I abuse him, he treats it as a jest; and when I rebuke him, he regards it as a familiarity granted by love.'

From all this you can easily gather how deeply in love the princess is. And I ask you, have you done well in leaving her in such a state?'

Hardly had Patralekha stopped speaking when a message arrived from Queen Vilasavati, summoning Chandrapida and Patralekha to her apartment. His mother's tenderness, far from soothing the prince, only increased his agitation. 'Alas, what shall I do!' he reflected, 'My dearest mother is sorrowful if I leave her even for a short while. The subjects love me, and my friends shower their affection upon me. And yet my mind is wholly taken up with thoughts of Kadambari. Everything seems harsh to me in her absence.'

As he was strolling on the bank of the Sipra river, lost in thought, he heard the clatter of hoofs. The horsemen approached closer and very soon he could make out the features of their leader. It was Keyuraka. He dismounted at a distance, came near the prince respectfully, and bowed to him. Chandrapida anxiously asked him if he had brought any message, and Keyuraka replied, 'Noble Prince, I bring no message. But I shall tell you what I saw. Mahashweta returned to her hermitage as soon she heard that you had suddenly taken the road to Ujjayini as for Kadambari, she merely gazed upon me with tearful eyes. She is enduring great torture and I have come here to tell you that she will not long survive the agony of her separation from you.'

Chandrapida made up his mind to visit Hemakuta before it was too late. And now he felt an intense longing to meet Vaishampayana Since the days of their childhood the two friends had shared each other's anxieties. They were accustomed to derive solace from one another's company in moments of agitation. Chandrapida sent Patralekha ahead, asking her to assure Kadambari that he would soon follow. And then he sent an urgent message to Vaishampayana, begging him to return as speedily as he could.

But after spending a sleepless night Chandrapida, without waiting for a reply to his message, himself started on the road to Dashapura. To his amazement he found that Vaishampayana was not present in the camp. He summoned one of the chieftains and asked him for news of Vaishampayana. The chieftain said, 'Alas, Vaishampayana is strangely distraught. We urged him to return to Ujjayini, but he refused. He has made up his mind to spend the rest of his life near the holy lake of Achchoda, occupying his mind solely in the worship of Siva. We left him in a pitiable state. His melancholy appearance baffled us.'

With a heavy heart Chandrapida returned to Ujjayini and sought his parents' permission to make another journey to the Himalayas in search of Vaishampayana. When he went to pay his respects to Vaishampayana's father, the latter expressed strong disapproval of his son's conduct. 'Men like Vaishampayana,' he said, 'are harbingers of evil. He did not fear the wrath of his king, nor did he give a moment's thought to his mother's condition. He was born only in order to cause grief.' When Shukanasa spoke in this vein, Chandrapida's father tried to pacify him. He said, 'Do not judge him so harshly in his absence. Let him be brought here first; then there will be time enough to censure him.'

Having obtained his parents' blessings, Chandrapida made ready to set out in search of Vaishampayana. The astrologers were not happy, but they tactfully said, 'The conjunction of the planets does not seem to favour your journey. But ultimately it is for the King to determine the auspicious moment for every undertaking.' But Chandrapida started, while Queen Vilasavati, who seemed to have a premonition of disaster, shed tears of grief.

The prince rode fast, and yet he had traversed only half the distance from Ujjayini to the Achchoda lake before the rainy season set in. All the terrors of storm and lightning found their counterpart in Chandrapida's own heart, so intense was his agitation. Impatiently brushing aside the advice of his companions, and giving no thought to bodily comfort, he continued his journey and reached the hermitage of Mahashweta.

He found Mahashweta at the entrance of the cave, supported by Taralika. She was weeping bitterly, and suffering had left deep marks upon her countenance. The prince thought: 'This is an evil portent indeed. I had hoped that she would express great joy at my arrival, but her sorrow seems to have been redoubled at my sight. God forbid that any ill should have befallen Kadambari.' Concealing his anxiety, Chandrapida asked Taralika how every one was faring. She silently pointed to Mahashweta, who unfolded a story as shameful as it was tragic.

XI

'When Keyuraka told me that you had left for Ujjayini,' Mahashweta said, 'My heart was weighed down by disappointment. You know how deep is my attachment to Kadambari, and how eager I was that she should find happiness through you. Your departure dashed my hopes to pieces, and I came here determined to undergo harsher penance than ever before.

Near the lake I saw a Brahmin youth.. The moment he set eyes upon me, he began to behave like one possessed. Though a perfect stranger, he dared to give me advice. He tried to turn me away from my ascetic life and said, 'fair maiden, why do you waste in such stern penance a body that is tender like a garland of jasmine buds? If you turn away from earthly joys, Cupid bends his bow in vain, and the moon casts its mellow light upon the horizon to no purpose.' I ignored his words and bade Taralika keep him at a distance. But he hovered around the hermitage, and I felt frightened.

One evening, while Taralika was asleep and I was thinking of Pundarika, the Brahmin youth approached me and said, 'O moon-faced maiden, I am being slain by the Moon, who is Cupid's ally. My life is in your hands. It is the duty of ascetics to grant protection to those who seek it. If you do not bestow yourself on me, I shall assuredly perish.' In a voice choking with anger I exclaimed: 'How is it, you wretch, that a thunderbolt did not strike you down as you uttered these words? It seems you do not possess the elements out of which the human frame is composed; otherwise earth, air, fire and water would have destroyed you for your wickedness. You have spoken like a parrot, without thought of right or wrong; and I lay upon you this curse: 'enter a birth suited to your speech'. Then I raised my eyes towards the moon and said, 'O Blessed Moon! If ever, since Pundarika left me, I have given a moment's thought to another man, let my curse fail. But if I have been faithful to his memory, let this false lover fall into a parrot-existence.'

As soon I uttered these syllables, the youth fell dead upon the ground. I do not know whether it was the power of my true love that destroyed him, or his own sins. He lay lifeless, like a tree uprooted from the earth. His attendants soon came looking for him and it was from them, dear Chandrapida, that I learnt with great sorrow that he was your friend, Vaishampayana.'

Chandrapida could not stand the shock of this revelation. The knowledge that his dearest friend was guilty of such discourtesy towards the saintly-natured Mahashweta caused him such acute shame that his heart sank and he collapsed. In a broken voice he muttered, 'Alas, I was not destined to see Kadambari!' And then the soul deserted his body. While Taralika was reproaching Mahashweta for her narration of Vaishampayana's folly, and while Chandrapida's followers were giving vent to bitter lamentation, Kadambari arrived there. She had come on the pretext of visiting Mahashweta and she was whispering into Patralekha's ears words of feigned anger, declaring that she would never speak to Chandrapida again even if he visited Hemakuta.

But when she saw him lying dead, she fell to the ground with a piercing cry. After a while she recovered consciousness and stood with quivering limbs, like a tender creeper under the blow of a sharp axe. Suddenly she stood erect, her gaze became steady, and her aspect acquired a firmness that was far more frightening than her agitation had been. Patralekha implored her to find an outlet for her grief in tears, lest her heart should break under the weight of her unnatural steadiness.

Kadambari replied, 'Foolish girl! How should my heart break now, having withstood such a sight? I have won the body of my beloved. Living or dead, it is enough to calm my grief. It is for me that he came here and lost his life. Shall I repay the great honour he has done me by shedding tears? And what sorrow is there now? The moment of our eternal union has arrived. Soon shall I join him in the land where no one can part us.'

Then, turning to her maid, Kadambari continued, 'Madalekha, see that the mango saplings I planted are properly tended. Let the *maina*, Kalindi, and the parrot, Parihasa, be freed from their cages. Let the sweet little mongoose that once rested in my lap now rest in yours. And see that my pleasure-hill is given as a gift to some calmsouled hermit. I shall now cling to my dear Lord's feet, and allay on the funeral pyre the fever that consumes my heart.'

With these words she bent down, lifted Chandrapida's feet, and placed them in her own lap. As soon as she did so, a mysterious light shot up from the Prince's body and a heavenly voice was heard to say, 'Mahashweta, once again I speak to you words of consolation. The body of Pundarika, nourished in my world, is awaiting reunion with you. The body of Chandrapida is also imperishable, having received the touch of Kadambari's hands. His soul has, by reason of a curse, momentarily taken leave of his body. You must preserve his frame carefully; let it not be burnt or cast into water. Kadambari and yourself must guard it until the curse ends.'

While every one gazed at the sky in wonder as the heavenly voice was heard, Patralekha unexpectedly seized Indrayudha from his groom and exclaimed, 'We may remain here, but you must join your master. How can he start on his long journey to Heaven without a steed?' With these words she plunged into the Achchoda lake, along with the horse. Immediately a young ascetic emerged from the lake and approached Mahashweta. 'Princess of the *Gandharvas*!' said the ascetic, 'do you not recognize me? I am Kapinjala, the friend and companion of Pundarika.'

Mahashweta bowed to him and said, 'Blessed Kapinjala, am I so deficient in virtue that I could ever forget you? And yet I cannot blame you if you think ill of me, since I continue to live even after Pundarika, the lord of my life, has gone to heaven. But enough of this. I am dying to know what has befallen you and your friend during this, period.'

Kapinjala said, 'As you know, when Pundarika was carried off by a heavenly being, I flew in hot pursuit. All the gods, sitting in their respective chariots, gaped in wonder as I followed the heavenly being through the sky. At last we reached the world of the moon, where the being laid Pundarika's body upon a couch and said, 'You must know, my friend, that I am the spirit of the moon. Once, when I was emerging on the horizon, Pundarika cursed me because my beams were causing him agony. The curse was that I should myself be subjected to the tortures of love on earth. At this I uttered a counter-curse that he and I should endure the same joys and sorrows. Later I came to know that he was in love with Mahashweta, whose race traces its origin to my beams. I was sorry that by cursing Pundarika I had unwittingly condemned Mahashweta to suffering. But now that cannot be helped. I have brought his body here, and I sustain it through the power of my light. I have tried to comfort Mahashweta. You must now go to Pundarika's father. He is a great sage, and might be able to find a way of neutralising the curse.'

As soon as the Moon stopped speaking, I rushed in search of Pundarika's father. Unfortunately, in my excitement I leapt over another heavenly being who was riding in a chariot. He was angry and pronounced this curse: 'Since you have leapt over me like a horse, may you be born as a horse on earth.' I pacified him and assured him that I had meant no discourtesy. He said, 'Well, the curse cannot be withdrawn. But I decree that when your rider dies you may be freed from the curse by bathing in a lake.'

I implored the heavenly being to arrange that in my existence as a horse I should be of service to Pundarika, who was destined to be born on earth along with the Moon. Touched by my affection, he told me that the Moon would be born as the son of King Tarapida of Ujjayini, Pundarika as the son of his minister, Shukanasa, and I would be the Prince's steed. That is how I came to be born as Indrayudha. I may now reveal that I deliberately brought Chandrapida here in pursuit of the *Kinnaras*. And if his friend, Vaishampayana, declared his love for you it was only because of the feelings implanted in his heart during his former birth as Pundarika.'

Having heard this sequence of events from Kapinjala, Mahashweta repented the harsh words she had said to Vaishampayana. 'Ah, Pundarika,' she exclaimed, 'you kept your love for me through another birth and I spurned you. It seems I have been granted a long life only to deprive you of life again and again!' Kapinjala said, 'Princess, you are not to be blamed. Now you must not grieve, but continue your penance. By the power of your austerities you shall soon be united with my friend.'

Kadambari asked Kapinjala what had become of Patralekha. He said he knew nothing of her fate. Then, bidding farewell to Mahashweta and Kadambari, he continued his journey in search of Pundarika's father, Shwetaketu.

Meanwhile, King Tarapida and Queen Vilasavati were exceedingly anxious for Chandrapida's welfare. At last, unable to bear the suspense, they travelled to Lake Achchoda, accompanied by Shukanasa and his wife. Queen Vilasavati broke into piteous lamentation when she saw the lifeless body of Chandrapida. By and by, the entire story of Chandrapida and the curse that had worked against him was made known to the King and Queen. They stayed on near the hermitage. And when they saw the prince's body growing brighter day by day, they felt cheered by the thought that he would regain consciousness and marry the princess of the *Gandharvas.*

Vilasavati said to Kadambari, 'Be of good cheer, my daughter-in-law. But for you, who could have looked after the body of my dearest child? Surely you must be composed entirely of *amrita,* that your touch has bestowed so much lustre on Chandrapida's countenance.' As for King Tarapida, he found his way of life entirely transformed in the forest. Instead of friends, he had fawns; instead of palaces, he had shady trees; and his silken robes were replaced by bark garments. But he put a cheerful countenance on his circumstances, and looked forward to the joy of seeing Chandrapida restored to life.

XII

The parrot continued: 'Such was the story unfolded by the sage, Jabali. When he had finished his narrative, he turned to his disciples and said, 'This is the lovesick youth who became Vaishampayana, son of Shukanasa. By his own fault, and by the power of Mahashweta's penance, he has now taken the form of a parrot. Just look at the gallant!'

I felt ashamed as all the events came back to me. A great yearning came over me to know what had happened to the Prince, to Mahashweta, and to Kadambari. I implored the sage to tell me about them. He looked at me scornfully and said, 'What! Even now you have not learnt to curb your impatience! Ask me when your wings are grown.'

One of the hermits took me to his hut and fed me. I was plunged in sorrow at the thought that years must elapse before the end of the curse. Just then Kapinjala reached the hermitage. He lifted me up with great tenderness, placed me on his shoulder, and said, 'Your father, Shwetaketu, has come to know of your plight through his divine insight. He has now begun a religious sacrifice to free you from your curse. Your mother, Lakshmi, is helping him in the rites. They send you their blessings and ask you to be patient.' With these words Kapinjala flew into the sky and rushed off to participate in the sacrifice.

After a few days, when my wings had grown, I could no longer bear my separation from Mahashweta and set off towards the Himalayas. But on the way I fell into the snare set by a *Chandala*. I entreated him to release me as I was on my way to meet my beloved; but he laughed at me. 'You are intended for the *Chandala* princess,' he said, 'She has heard of your gifts and wants to keep you as a pet.' And so I, the son of a great sage, was cast among a tribe whom even barbarians treat with contempt.

The hard-hearted *Chandala* carried me to his settlement. What an evil place! The people who lived there were clothed in horrible attire. They were unleashing their hounds, training their falcons or mending their snares. They thought of nothing but hunting. The enclosures of their huts were made of skulls, and on the roads there were enormous heaps of bones.

The *Chandala* princess put me in a cage, and said, 'I shall tame him all right. Let him show his wilfulness here!' But when I refused all food for a few days, she spoke to me tenderly. 'Don't be stupid, little parrot,' she said. 'It is unnatural for living creatures to spurn food. It is no use thinking of a former birth. You are now an animal, and the laws of animal life demand that nourishment should be imbibed.' I was surprised at her wisdom and obeyed her.

After many months, when I had become a full-grown parrot, I woke up one day to find myself in this golden cage. The entire barbarian settlement looked like a city of gods. The *Chandala* maiden was dressed in gorgeous clothes. I marvelled at the transformation, but before I could ask what it all meant I was brought into your august presence.

Such is the story of my life as a parrot and of my former birth. I have related everything that I remembered. I do not know what the future holds, nor can l imagine why I have been brought to your palace.'

XIII

King Shudraka heard the parrot's story with amazement. When the parrot ceased speaking, the king sent for the *Chandala* maiden and asked her who she was. The maiden said, 'You, Oh Moon, have heard the story of your own past birth. You have also heard of Vaishampayana, who is the same as Pundarika, and who is at present living as a parrot. I must now reveal that I am no. *Chandala* woman; I am Lakshmi, the mother of this Vaishampayana. I brought him here so that he might be saved from his own impatience until the sacrifice undertaken by his father is safely over. His curse is about to end. Now may you both leave your mortal bodies.' With these words she vanished into the sky.

The king remembered his former birth and said, 'Dear Pundarika, let us rejoice that both of us are about to be released from the curse simultaneously.' But even as he uttered these words, Cupid twanged his bow with deadly effect, and the Moon fell desperately in love with Kadambari. Meanwhile Kadambari herself was guarding the body of Chandrapida with great devotion. When the day of the Spring Festival arrived, she anointed it with sandal paste and decked it with flowers. Then, unable to restrain herself, she embraced Chandrapida.

Suddenly the prince regained consciousness, clasped her closely, and said, 'Dearest Kadambari, your embrace has revived me. I have now left the body of King Shudraka and come back to you. Vaishampayana, too, has been liberated from his curse.' While the Moon, or Chandrapida, spoke thus, Pundarika descended from the sky, accompanied by Kapinjala. With great joy Kadambari informed Mahashweta of their advent. Finally King Tarapida and Queen Vilasavati, together with Shukanasa and his wife, joined the two couples. And so happiness came to all of them.

One day Kadambari asked her husband, 'How is it that, while all of us have been reunited, no one knows what has happened to Patralekha?' The prince replied: 'How could Patralekha be here, dearest Kadambari? She is none other than my wife, Rohini. When I was cursed, and became Chandrapida instead of the Moon, she grieved for me and descended in the world of mortals to serve me. She has now returned to the heavenly home.' Kadambari stood speechless when she heard of Rohini's selfless devotion and loftiness.

Chandrapida, following his father's example, gave up his kingdom. He entrusted the affairs of state to Pundarika, and began to divide his time between Hemakuta and Ujjayini. Sometimes, out of his affection for Rohini, he would also visit the world of the Moon; and sometimes Pundarika would invite him to the dwelling-place of his mother, Lakshmi. And, as Chandrapida enjoyed an eternity of bliss in the company of Kadambari, so did Pundarika reach the pinnacle of happiness with his beloved Mahashweta.

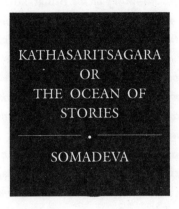

KATHASARITSAGARA
OR
THE OCEAN OF
STORIES

·

SOMADEVA

Somadeva *lived in Kashmir in the latter half of the eleventh century. He tells us that, when he wrote the stories of* Kathasaritsagara, *Kashmir was governed by King Ananta, 'whose footstool was like a touchstone for testing the worth of the jewels in the crowns of all the monarchs who bowed before him'. He extols the beauty and generosity of Ananta's wife, Suryamati. Disclaiming all originality,* Somadeva *describes his work as merely the distilled essence of the* Brihatkatha, *or the 'Great Tale', said to have been composed by* Gunadhya. *'In order to divert, if only for a short while, the mind of that gracious* queen, Suryamati, this summary of the Brihatkatha has been written by Soma, the son of Rama, a worthy and virtuous Brahmin.'

It was a confused, contradictory age, particularly for Kashmir. Great achievements in poetry, architecture and even philosophy went hand in hand with political disintegration and intellectual debasement. The air was thick with intrigue. Somadeva was himself a witness to tragic events at the court—conspiracy, usurpation, suicide and bloodshed. Old ideals were crumbling. All kinds of esoteric cults had emerged, dragging the human mind into superstition and unreason. These contradictions are clearly reflected in Kathasaritsagara. We find here much that is tender and elevating; but we also come upon the ruthless and depressing side of life.

The most striking quality of the 'Ocean of Stories' is its stupendous range. It is unquestionably the largest single collection of stories in the world, being twice as big as the Iliad and the Odyssey put together. The title of the work is no idle boast. The Kathasaritsagara is indeed a mighty ocean, uniting in itself all the rivers of myth, mystery, fact, fancy, legend, tradition and romance that had 'flowed' in India since time immemorial.

The comparison is apt from another point of view. Rivers begin as tiny streams. The further they move from their source, the more they swell. Likewise, stories that have been told and retold for centuries no longer remain episodic. They grow, their course becomes wide, they become powerful forces of cultural transmission. They irrigate vast tracts of the human consciousness. In Somadeva's great classic it is not the tiny streams but these mighty currents that have been gathered together.

But perhaps we can vary the metaphor and describe the 'Ocean of Stories' as a vast picture-gallery in which men and women are depicted filling a variety of roles in the drama of life. Some of them face unusual situations and cross into the magic realm of the supernatural. Others find adventure through more normal channels.

Still others live out their lives swayed by the longings, passions, hopes and disappointments that are the common lot of all men. And the marvel is that in spite of this endless diversity of character and situation, in spite of the gigantic scale on which the entire work is conceived, the aesthetic unity is never seriously disturbed.

KING
BRAHMADATTA
AND THE
GOLDEN SWANS

N

o other city on earth has attained such imperishable renown as Varanasi which, like the body of Siva, is adorned by the holy Ganga. The flags of its myriad temples sway in the wind and seem to beckon to men, saying: 'Come, attain salvation here!'

In this great city of Varanasi there once ruled a king named Brahmadatta—a patron of learned men, full of generosity and compassion, of dauntless courage, and wholly devoted to Siva. His commands were obeyed everywhere. They suffered no barriers of sea or mountain. In every continent his word was law.

King Brahmadatta had a queen, Somaprabha, who was as dear
to him as the lotus is to the sun. And he had a Brahmin minister named
Sivabhuti who had fathomed the meaning of the scriptures and whose
intellect was unsurpassed in brilliance and acumen. Thus King
Brahmadatta, enjoying the love of his beautiful queen, and profiting
by the counsel of his loyal minister, spent his days happily.

Once, as the king was lying on his terrace in the moonlight, he
saw two swans flying close by. Their bodies were of gleaming gold,
and they looked like fresh lotuses in the heavenly Ganga. The king
gazed upon them with admiring eyes; and when they faded into the
distance he became exceedingly sad. Sleep eluded him. He longed for
a repetition of the sight.

Next morning he sent for his minister and, after describing what
he had seen, said, 'My friend, it·has become absolutely necessary for
me to feast my eyes once again upon those golden swans. If I cannot
do so, neither my kingdom nor my life has any worth in my estimate.
Muster all your resourcefulness and see that my heart's desire is
fulfilled.'

Sivabhuti said, 'Sir, do not be anxious. I have thought of a plan
already. Providence has ordained that every living species should find
pleasure in particular types of food, drink and dwelling-place. Swans
are no exception. Let us construct a pleasant artificial lake, covered
with various kinds of lotuses; and let suitable food be scattered on the
banks of this lake. Very soon we shall tempt the golden swans into
your presence.'

Acting on the minister's advice, the king had a delightful pool
built outside the city. Within a few days the guards came and informed
him that the pair of golden swans had arrived and made themselves at
home on a clump of lotuses. The king hastened to the pool and great
was his delight as he saw those lovely birds. He admired them from a
distance and looked to their comfort. Large quantities of rice, dipped

in milk, were scattered on the banks; and the guards were ordered to take every precaution so that no one might molest the swans. The king spent most of his time watching them. Their bodies were golden like the setting sun, their eyes bright like pearls, their beaks and feet were coral-red, and the tips of their wings were emerald-green.

One day, as the king was strolling by the lakeside, he saw a place where an offering of fresh flowers had been made. As there was no shrine in the vicinity, he was surprised and asked the guards about it. One of the guards said, 'Your Majesty, thrice every day—at dawn, noon and sunset—these golden swans bathe in the lake and, having purified themselves, make an offering of flowers. Then they stand devoutly, as though absorbed in meditation. Such a wonder has never been seen or heard of.'

The king was amazed at this report. So great was his curiosity that he decided to perform severe penance in order to know the truth about these swans. So he gave up food and water, and worshipped Siva with all his heart. After the king had fasted for twelve days the two heavenly swans came to him in a dream and said, 'Arise, noble King! We are touched by your eagerness to know our story. Tomorrow morning, after you have broken your fast, we shall reveal the truth.'

So early next morning the king, the queen and the minister sat in a pleasure pavilion near the pool and, having partaken of food, awaited the swans. The birds kept their promise and related their history.

And this is what they said.

* * *

The whole world knows about Mount Mandara, the monarch of all mountains. In its gleaming groves all the gods and goddesses of heaven roam for pleasure. On its slopes, irrigated with nectar, there are flowers and fruits that are antidotes to old age and death. Its highest peak, abounding in precious gems, serves as Siva's pleasure-ground. Indeed, he loves it even more than Kailasa.

On this glorious Mount Mandara, Siva one day left Parvati and went away on some business of the gods. Then gentle Parvati, lonely in his absence, wandered from spot to spot recalling pleasant memories. She felt sad, and all the other gods tried to console her.

When spring arrived, Parvati was all the more afflicted by her separation from Siva. One day she was sitting pensively under a tree, thinking about her beloved Lord. Her servants were near her, waiting to fulfil her wishes instantly. Now among these attendants there was a young maiden called Chandralekha who was waving a fan over Parvati's head. As her shapely arm moved gracefully from left to right, her maidenly charm attracted another attendant, Manipushpesvara. He was a match for her in youth and beauty. As he stood by her side, and his glance told her that he was smitten by her loveliness, Chandralekha responded with a tender expression in her eyes.

Two other servants, Pingesvara and Guhesvara, saw what had happened. They exchanged glances, and a smile passed over their lips. When Parvati saw them smiling, she was offended. She turned round and saw that Chandralekha and Manipushpesvara were looking at each other with unconcealed passion. Distracted as she was with the sorrow of separation, the goddess became angry. She thought that her servants had been guilty of unseemly conduct in her presence. She exclaimed in a tone of impatience, 'So, when their master is away these young people make love to each other! And these other two amuse themselves by watching their faces! Very well, let these two lovers, blinded with passion, fall into a human birth. They shall be man and wife. But these impudent watchers shall endure many miseries. They shall live as poor Brahmins, than as *Rakshasas,* then *Pisachas,* and then as *Chandalas.* After that they shall be born among robbers, and then they shall pass through animal existences. They shall become dogs, and then birds.

That will teach them to laugh in my presence!'

All her attendants were horrified at the severity of this curse. One of them, Dhurjata by name, said, 'Mighty Goddess, you are being extremely unjust. These poor servants do not deserve such dire punishment for such a small offence.' At this Parvati uttered another curse and ordained that Dhurjata, too, should be born as a mortal.

After a while, when her anger was somewhat pacified, Chandralekha's mother clung to her feet and implored her to soften the curse. Parvati relented and said, 'Well, perhaps you are right. It was through ignorance that these wretches behaved in this way. When all these, having obtained insight, shall in course of time gather together they shall return to our court. You may also rest assured that Chandralekha and her beloved, and also the well-meaning Dhurjata, shall lead happy lives as mortals. But as for the two who laughed in my presence, I insist that they shall be miserable.' As soon as Parvati ceased speaking, the five attendants descended to earth.

Now listen to the history of Pingesvara and Guhesvara.

* * *

In the village of Yajnasthala there lived a rich and virtuous Brahmin named Yajnasoma. Somewhat late in life two sons were born to him. The elder was named Harisoma and the younger Devasoma. Their childhood was spent happily enough, and they were duly invested with the sacred thread. But after that they fell on dark days. The Brahmin lost all his wealth and soon departed from life. His wife did not long survive him. The two orphans were left without subsistence. Relatives soon deprived them of whatever was left, and they were reduced to living on alms. So they decided to take shelter with their maternal grandfather who lived in another village.

They proceeded by slow stages, begging their way, but when they reached the village they discovered that their grandfather and grandmother were also dead. Tired after their journey, and covered with dust from head to foot, they somehow located the house of their maternal uncles, Yajnadeva and Kratudeva. These two Brahmins welcomed them and gave them food and clothing. But in course of time their wealth, too, dwindled through a series of misfortunes. They had to dismiss their servants and cut down their establishment.

One day, when their income ceased almost entirely, they said to their nephews, 'Dear boys, our condition is known to you. We can no longer keep a man to look after our cattle. So you will have to help us.'

Harisoma and Devasoma took up the work assigned to them. Every morning they took the cattle to the forest, looked after them all day, and in the evening returned home utterly exhausted. They were, after all, small boys. Sometimes they would fall asleep and animals would be stolen or dragged away by tigers. One day a cow and a goat intended for a religious sacrifice disappeared. Weighed down with shame and fear, the boys brought the other animals home before the usual time and returned to the jungle in search of the missing cow and goat. In a remote part of the forest they discovered the goat, half eaten by a tiger. Long did they lament, and ultimately decided not to return home. They thought: 'This goat was meant for a holy sacrifice. If we tell our uncles that it has been devoured by a tiger they will be angry. Let us wander off to some other village and somehow support ourselves by begging. Meanwhile let us satisfy our hunger tonight by cooking whatever is left of this goat.'

As they proceeded to roast the goat, their uncles arrived. They were furious when they saw the two boys sitting around a fire on which portions of the goat were being cooked. The boys were terrified and, without giving any explanation, fled from the spot. The two uncles thundered at them, "Ungrateful wretches, is this how you repay us for our hospitality? In your longing for flesh you have done something which is worthy only of *Rakshasas*. We curse you: 'May you become flesh-eating *Rakshasas*.' "

As soon as the curse was pronounced Harisoma and Devasoma were transformed into *Rakshasas*, with formidable jaws and flaming hair. They also acquired a prodigious appetite, and they roamed the forest, catching and eating animals. One day they rushed upon an ascetic who possessed supernatural power. The ascetic, in self-defence, cursed them. As a result of this curse they became *Pisachas*. In their condition as *Pisachas* they once tried to carry off a cow that belonged to a holy Brahmin. They were overpowered by the Brahmin's spells and were reborn as *Chandalas*.

One day, tormented with hunger, they were roaming about in the countryside and happened to enter a village of bandits. The village guards, taking them for thieves, arrested them and cut off their ears and noses. They were bound with stout ropes, belaboured with sticks, and hauled up before the chief of the bandits. When they related their history the chief was moved to pity and said, 'Remain with us. We shall supply you with food. You have arrived here on the eighth day of the month—the day on which we worship Kartikeya. You are our guests. You shall share in our feast.' And so the two *Chandalas* stayed on in the village. By and by the bandits took a fancy to them. They displayed great courage during raids and eventually became the chiefs of the gang.

Many days later they raided a large town which was a favourite abode of Siva himself. Evil omens were ignored and they plundered the holy city, including the temple of Siva. The inhabitants prayed for protection and the mighty God bewildered the bandits by depriving them of sight. The citizens realized that it was Siva who had made their enemies blind. The chiefs were captured and beaten, while many of the followers were put to death.

The two chiefs were about to be killed when they were

miraculously transformed into dogs. In this condition they suddenly remembered their former birth, and their delusion vanished. In order to put an end to their curse they fasted and tried to pacify Siva by severe asceticism. The citizens who came to worship at the shrine offered them food but the creatures would not touch it. The two dogs remained in this condition for a long time, and then the attendants of Siva on holy Kailasa implored their master to take pity on their two former companions. They said, 'Mercy, Oh greatest of Gods! Your former servants, Pingesvara and Guhesvara, who were cursed by the Goddess in a moment of anger, have suffered great miseries for a long time. Please take pity on them.' Siva ordained that they should be delivered from their canine condition and become crows. So Pingesvara and Guhesvara were transformed into crows. They broke their fast on the grains of rice that lay scattered on the temple floor. And they continued their devotion to Siva.

After some time they became vultures, and then peacocks. And finally the two were born as swans. In this condition they showed even greater devotion to Siva. They gained Siva's favour by bathing in sacred pools and by many acts of worship. Their bodies became golden and they attained supernatural insight.

* * *

King Brahmadatta, Queen Somaprabha and the counsellor Sivabhuti had listened to the swans with silent reverence. When their narrative ended, the king paid homage to them. But as he was about to say something the swans cut him short and said, 'Oh King, you must know that we ourselves are those two attendants of Siva who, having endured a succession of miseries through Parvati's curse, have now become swans and are speaking to you at this moment. And you must know that Manipushpesvara, who fell in love with Chandralekha when she was waving a fan over Parvati's head, has become a king upon this mortal earth; and that king is none other than yourself, Brahmadatta. Further, Chandralekha has been born as a queen, and she is none other than your own wife, Somaprabha. Finally, we must tell you that Dhurjata, who tried to intercede on our behalf and earned Parvati's anger, has been born as your minister, Shivabhuti, who is with us just now.

You will now understand why we, having already attained insight, and remembering the promised end of Parvati's curse, appeared to you in a dream. We have now all been reunited here and all three of you will soon attain perfection of insight.'

As soon as the swans stopped speaking, King Brahmadatta, his wife, and his minister all attained supernatural knowledge. They also immediately acquired the power of flying through the air. Accompanied by the two golden swans, they flew to Siddhisvara on the Tridasha mountain, and prayed to Siva. They laid aside the bodies into which they had entered and.were reinstated in their former position as servants of Siva and Parvati.

And Parvati, being in a cheerful mood, welcomed them with words of tenderness and affection.

HOW MADANASENA KEPT HER PROMISE

When Virabahu was the King of Anangapura, there lived in that city a prosperous merchant named Arthadatta. He had two children—a son named Dhanadatta, and a daughter, a veritable pearl among maidens, who was called Madanasena.

One day as Madanasena was playing with her companions in a garden, a young man named Dharmadatta saw her. As soon as he set eyes on her he was robbed of his senses. Cupid seemed to have showered upon him all his flowery arrows. When Madanasena left the garden, Dharmadatta was immersed in the gloom of separation. The setting sun seemed to be inflamed with the fire of grief at Madanasena's departure. And the moon slowly mounted upwards, having made sure that his rival in beauty was no longer outside her room.

Dharmadatta went home and tossed in his bed. He was restless. Sleep refused his eager invitations. His friends and relations questioned him about the cause of his dejection, but he kept silent. In the morning he went to the garden once again and saw Madanasena sitting under a tree. As she was alone, he went up to her and declared his love in words surcharged with passion. She replied that she had been betrothed to another. 'My father has announced my engagement to the merchant Samudragupta,' she said. 'I shall be married in a few days, and cannot now be yours even if I had loved you. Please leave me and let no one see you.'

But Dharmadatta was like one in delirium. 'Happen what may,' he said, 'I cannot live without you.' His passion frightened her. Since they were together in a secluded part of the garden she feared that he might do something rash. So, in order to get rid of him for the time being, she said, 'Let my marriage be celebrated first. And then I shall visit you, for your devotion has won me over.'

But how can a man in love endure the thought that his beloved should visit him only after being embraced by another? Dharmadatta said, 'You have promised to visit me, and I shall hold you to it. But you must come before you live with your husband. How can a bee take delight in a lotus on which another bee has settled?'

Madanasena was rash enough to give this further assurance as well. Then he let her go and she returned home in great agitation.

The auspicious day arrived. The wedding was celebrated. Madanasena went to her husband's house and spent the day in great merriment. But when evening came she would not respond to her husband's advances. When he began to coax her she burst into tears. The husband, being a man of great sympathy, said, 'Fair one, if you do not love me, I don't want you. Go to the man of your choice, whoever he may be.'

With downcast eyes Madanasena said, 'l love you more than my own life. But I am caught up in a terrible situation. Promise not to be angry and I shall tell you.' Her husband promised to listen patiently and she told him what had happened in the garden. 'l must keep my word,' she continued, 'l have not transgressed the law of truth even as a child. Will you ask me to do so now? Let me pay a visit to that young man. When I return to you my mind will be at ease, as I shall have kept my promise. And please do not doubt my great love for you.'

These words hit Samudradatta like a thunderbolt. The idea that his wife should visit another man on the very day of his marriage oppressed him sorely. But he permitted her to go.

The moon ascended the great eastern mountain as if it were the roof of a palace. The Nymph of the East smiled, as though touched by the moon's fingers. The Spirit of Darkness was still embracing the shrubs in the forest. At this time, while Madanasena was going alone at night, a thief surprised her. 'Who are you and where are you going?' he asked, seizing her by the hem of her garment.

Madanasena was terrified. But, somehow overcoming her agitation, she said, 'What is that to you? Let me go. I have to meet someone for an urgent reason.'

'Let you go!' the thief exclaimed. 'Don't you see that I am a thief?'

'Very well, then. Take my jewels and leave me alone.'

'What shall I do with these ornaments? I shall not surrender you, the ornament of the earth. Your face is like the moonstone. Your feet are like rubies, and your limbs are more precious than gold and diamonds.'

Madanasena now took the thief into her confidence and narrated her story. 'Let me keep my word,' she pleaded. 'After visiting Dharmadatta I shall return to you. Believe me, I shall not break my promise. Remain here till I fulfil my commitment.'

She spoke these words with such earnestness that the thief actually believed her. So he allowed her to go, and remained at that spot awaiting her. Madanasena went to Dharmadatta who had, in the meanwhile, begun to feel ashamed of his blind passion for another man's wife. When he saw her coming to the forest all alone by night, he felt all the more guilty. 'I am touched by your faithfulness to your promise,' he said, 'You are the wife of another, and I have no claims upon you. Please forgive me and go back to your husband's house.'

Having kept her word with Dharmadatta, she returned to the place where the thief was waiting for her. 'What happened?' he asked. 'Did you keep your tryst?' Madanasena told him exactly what had taken place.

It was now the thief's turn to be struck with wonder and admiration for her courage. 'It is true that I am a thief,' he said. 'But I am also a human being. Your truthfulness has touched my heart. I do not want either your ornaments or yourself. Go home. May you be happy with your husband .'

Madanasena returned to her husband's home and told him how she had kept her word and also preserved her honour. Samudragupta, convinced that his extraordinary wife would not have hesitated to tell the truth even if she had lost her chastity, believed her. He welcomed her to his arms with great affection.

And so Madanasena, having kept two rash promises, began to live happily with her considerate husband.

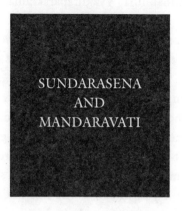

SUNDARASENA
AND
MANDARAVATI

I n the country of Nishadha
there is a famous city named Alaka. Since ancient times it has been
known for the wealth of its inhabitants and the grandeur of its
buildings. In this city of Alaka there once ruled King Mahasena. The
name of his chief queen was Shashiprabha, and she bore him a son
whom they called Sundarasena.

The prince grew up into a brilliant and courageous youth. He
mastered all the arts of war and peace. The citizens doted upon him.
Fortunately he had five companions, all of noble birth and all his equals
in courage and resourcefulness. The names of these friends were

Chandaprabha, Bhimabhuja, Vyaghraparakrama, Vikramashakti and Dridhabuddhi.

One day the prince, accompanied by his five companions, went out on a hunting expedition. On the outskirts of the city he was greeted by a female mendicant named Katyayani. She hailed him and offered her blessings, but the prince was so much engrossed in conversation that he did not hear her. Katyayani was annoyed. She approached Sundarasena and said, 'Are you too great even to accept my blessings? Don't you know that I, Katyayani, receive the respectful attention of every monarch on earth? If you are so proud now, what will happen to you if you obtain a wife like Mandaravati! I suppose you will not listen to even Siva or Indra.'

Sundarasena apologized to the ascetic and touched her feet. He said, 'Revered mother, please forgive me. I was absentminded. Indeed, who has not heard of you? But tell me, who is this Mandaravati that you mentioned?'

Katyayani was mollified. She smiled and said 'Young man, this Mandaravati is every whit your match in beauty. She is the daughter of King Mandaradeva of Hamsadvipa, who is convinced that there is no prince in the entire world worthy to become his son-in-law. In the course of my wanderings I once visited Hamsadvipa and saw the princess. She is like another moon composed entirely of nectar. But why should I waste words? Here is her picture which I drew when I saw her.' With these words she opened her bag and unrolled a piece of canvas. As soon as Sundarasena saw the portrait he was pierced by Cupid's flowery arrow. He was wrapt in admiration; and, watching that picture, he himself became motionless like one painted on a canvas.

One of Sundarasena's friends, sceptical of the mendicant's skill, said, 'Mother, will you kindly paint a picture of our friend, the Prince?' Katyayani immediately complied with the request. She pulled out another piece of canvas from her bag and within a few moments drew a wonderful likeness of Sundarasena. All the friends were now convinced that Princess Mandaravati must indeed be as lovely as her picture.

When the prince returned home he entered the inner chamber clasping the picture of Mandaravati. He had fallen desperately in love. 'Can it indeed be the face of a girl?' he mused. 'Or is it merely a picture of the moon with its dark spot removed?' The more he looked at that fair countenance, the more intense became his longing to see the original. He shut himself up in his room and, refusing all nourishment, was soon utterly exhausted by the fever of love.

His friends informed King Mahasena of what had happened. The king approached Sundarasena and said, 'My son, why do you conceal your feelings? There is nothing to be ashamed about. Mandaravati is a pearl among maidens. She will be a good match for you. Moreover, I know her father, Mandaradeva. Why torment yourself about something which can be easily arranged through an ambassador?' And so the king despatched a trusted envoy to Hamsadvipa.

The envoy, whose name was Surathadeva, carried with him the portrait of Sundarasena executed by Katyayani. Travelling as fast as he could, he reached the city of Shashankapura on the seashore. There he met King Mahendraditya, one of Mahasena's allies, who placed at his disposal a ship for the subsequent journey to Hamsadvipa. After a long voyage, Surathadeva reached the island of Hamsadvipa and announced himself in the palace of King Mandaradeva.

When the ambassador conveyed the proposal of marriage, the king was delighted. He sent for his wife and daughter. They unrolled the canvas and looked at the portrait. The king immediately discarded his former notion that no suitable match could be found for his daughter. He said, 'My daughter's beauty will not go in vain if she weds this prince. They will complete each other, like the swan and the lotus-bed.'

Meanwhile the princess had swooned away through excess of love as soon as she had set her eyes on the picture. She was carried to the inner apartments and nursed back into consciousness. Her father assured her that her desire would be fulfilled. He sent his own ambassador, a Brahmin named Kumaradatta, to convey to King Mahasena his acceptance of the proposal.

The city of Alaka rejoiced when the prince's engagement was announced. Astrologers were sent for and asked to name a suitable date for the wedding. They studied the horoscopes of Sundarasena and Mandaravati and declared that an auspicious date would present itself after three months, on the fifth day of the bright fortnight in the month of *kartika*. A messenger was again sent to Hamsadvipa and the date of the wedding was announced.

Every day that dawned saw Mandaravati more deeply in love than ever. The fire of separation scorched her. Sandalwood ointment was, to her limbs, a shower of hot coals. Her couch of lotus leaves was, to her, like a burning sand-bed. The rays of the moon were like the pointed flames of a forest fire. At last, unable to endure her separation from her betrothed, she declared that she would put an end to her life.

Her parents saw her condition with deep anxiety. After prolonged deliberation they said, 'After all, King Mahasena of Alaka is on good terms with us. Why should we allow our daughter to suffer like this? Let her go to Alaka and remain near her beloved, so that she may be able to endure the delay.' Having come to this conclusion King Mandaradeva comforted his daughter. A beautiful ship was made ready, luxuriously furnished, and placed in the hands of an expert captain. Mandaravati set out for Alaka. Her escort was Vinitamati, one of the trusted ministers of King Mandaradeva.

The ship sailed smoothly for a few days. And then fate took an evil turn. A mighty, dark cloud, yelling like a bandit, descended upon the ship. The gale dragged the ship, struck it with terrible force and broke it into pieces. Vinitamati was drowned, all the treasure was lost, and the crew were never heard of again. But the sea lifted up the princess and deposited her in a secluded spot on the shore. Terrified and confused, Mandaravati emerged from the sea only to fall into the deeper ocean of grief. She wept copiously, and her tears fell from her eyes like the pearls of a broken necklace.

After a while, a hermit named Matanga came that way for his bath. He was accompanied by his daughter, Yamuna, who had taken a vow of celibacy. They were deeply moved at the sight of Mandaravati who looked helpless like a doe separated from a herd of deer. Feeling reassured by their kindness, Mandaravati told them her story. The hermit fondly took her to his hermitage and made her comfortable in every way. In the company of Yamuna, Mandaravati was able to bear with her fate. She remained there leading an ascetic life and waiting upon the sage. But her future husband, whom she had never seen, was in her thoughts all the time.

As the date recommended by the astrologers approached, Prince Sundarasena and his friends started for Hamsadvipa. They stopped for a while at Shashankapura on the seashore, where King Mahendraditya welcomed them. When Prince Sundarasena rode through the streets of Shashankapura, the splendour of his face shook the hearts of all the fair maidens as a hurricane shakes lotus-buds. The prince spent the night in King Mahendraditya's magnificent palace. But he did not get a moment's sleep, so engrossed was his mind in the image of Mandaravati. Next morning he left his army in the city and started on the voyage to Hamsadvipa in a large ship well supplied with food and water. King Mahendraditya accompanied him.

After three days a terrible storm suddenly descended upon them. Even the forest on the shore shook this way and that, as if expressing its astonishment at the fury of the gale. Mighty sea-waves were turned upside down by the wind, as affections are inverted by the passage of time. Cries of terror rose from the cabins. Costly jewels were offered up to the sea, but the elements were not pacified. At last, when there was no further hope of saving the ship, the prince and his companions jumped into the sea. King Mahendraditya followed them. They were all expert swimmers; but the force of the waves scattered them in different directions. Prince Sundarasena and Dridhabuddhi luckily reached an abandoned ship and managed to climb upon it. After a while the wind fell and the sea became hushed, like a good man whose anger is appeased. The ship on which the prince and his friend had found shelter was gently wafted by the breeze to a distant part of the shore. There it stuck fast. The two companions jumped on dry land and their life was saved.

The prince fell into a state of deep depression. 'Alas, my good friend Dridhabuddhi,' he said, 'We have escaped from the sea—but what is left to us now? All our companions are drowned; so is King Mahendraditya, who had joined us through pure courtesy. How shall my father endure his grief for me? And what will Mandaravati think when I fail to turn up on the day fixed for our wedding?' Dridhabuddhi consoled him as much as he could, and the two friends began to look for fruits to sustain themselves.

As they were entering the forest, they met two hermits who were going towards the sea for their bath. The hermits befriended them and invited them to their hermitage. Sundarasena and Dridhabuddhi settled down there, and derived comfort from the company of holy men.

Meanwhile, Bhimabhuja and Vikramashakti, having swam across, reached the shore at a place several miles away. They entered the great forest, and wandered in search of their leader. The remaining two friends, Chandaprabha and Vyaghraparakrama, also escaped from the sea, along with King Mahendraditya. They found that the ship, though damaged, was still seaworthy; and so they set sail for Shashankapura. The king returned sorrowfully to his palace, while the two friends proceeded to Alaka. When King Mahasena and his queen heard of the disaster that had befallen their son, they gave themselves up to bitter lamentation. It was with the greatest difficulty that their ministers prevented them from ending their lives. The king, however, retired from affairs of state. He began to lead an ascetic life in a temple of Siva outside the city.

Mandaravati's parents, too, were prostrated with grief when they heard of their daughter's disappearance after the shipwreck. King Mandaradeva entrusted his realm to loyal ministers and started for Alaka. He joined his partner in misfortune, and the two kings remained together in the temple, united by their common sorrow. They practised severe austerities in the hope of appeasing the wrath of the gods.

One day, as Sundarasena was wandering about in the forest, chance brought him to the hermitage of Matanga. There was a lake of crystal-clear water near the hermitage, and on the bank of the lake there were trees laden with luscious fruits. The prince refreshed himself with a bath and ate some of the fruits. As he was resting under a tree he saw some hermit maidens gathering flowers. He went closer and saw that one of the maidens was a peerless beauty. She seemed to illumine the entire forest with her loveliness.

The prince was amazed to see that the maiden bore a close resemblance to Mandaravati, whose picture he carried in his eyes. He said to his friend, 'Dridhabuddhi, what marvel is this? Is she a nymph from heaven, or is she the presiding deity of this forest? And have you not noticed that she looks just like Mandaravati! But perhaps my distracted imagination is making sport of me. Mandaravati is in Hamsadvipa, far away!'

Sundarasena's reflexions were interrupted by a terror-stricken scream that came from the direction of the maidens. The two friends rushed there. They saw the peerless beauty being dragged away by a crocodile. The maidens cried, 'Help, help! Oh woodland gods, save our dearest Mandaravati.'

These words were like nectar to Sundarasena's ears. He rushed forward and killed the crocodile with a dagger. Mandaravati escaped unhurt. When she got over her fear, she reflected: 'Who is this hero that has appeared in the forest from nowhere and saved my life? And how amazing that he should look so much like my beloved Sundarasena! But heaven forbid! Why should the prince be exiled from his native land on the eve of our wedding?' With these thoughts she turned to one of her friends and said modestly, 'Thank this noble gentleman on my behalf and take leave of him respectfully. We must return to the hermitage.'

The prince now revealed his identity. As soon as Mandaravati heard that he was indeed the prince to whom she was engaged, she fainted through sheer excess of joy. The prince sprinkled cool water upon her face and fanned her back into consciousness. The two embraced each other, and even the herbs and flowers melted into tears at the sight of their union.

The maidens rushed to the hermitage and informed Matánga of what had happened. He came and comforted Sundarasena. 'My son,' he said, 'I am sure that all your misfortunes will be over. You shall return to Alaka and reign happily for many years. You must cherish this maiden tenderly; she is like a daughter to me.' Sundarasena and Mandaravati, though still grief-stricken through their separation from their parents, began to live in the hermitage. They sustained themselves with the hope that some day they would return to Alaka and get married.

A few days later, as the two of them, accompanied by Dridhabuddhi, were walking about near the shore, they saw a ship. They waved and the ship approached the shore. Sundarasena thought that he must not miss this chance of returning to Alaka. He persuaded the owner of the ship, a young and wealthy merchant, to give them a passage.

Now this merchant was wicked and cunning. At the sight of Mandaravati, his passion was roused. Concealing his designs, he agreed to take all three of them on his ship. But as soon as Mandaravati had climbed up, he pushed the other two down and set sail. Sundarasena wept helplessly as the ship moved away and Mandaravati's piteous cries faded into the distance.

Dridhabuddhi tried to encourage him to adopt a manly course. 'Arise, and stop this weeping and wailing,' he said. 'Is your conduct worthy of a hero? We must travel quickly through the forest and somehow secure help so that this brigand may be intercepted. In the hour of calamity we must not remain idle.' And so the two friends hastened through the forest, hoping to find some human habitation at the other end. Now and again Sundarasena would be overwhelmed with the grief of separation. Whenever he saw creepers in full bloom he was reminded of Mandaravati. In the songs of the cuckoos he heard the sweet voice of his beloved. He longed to linger at every beautiful spot and give himself up to brooding, but his friend urged him on.

When the two friends had almost reached the end of the forest another misfortune overtook them. Certain members of the Pulinda tribe, who were on the look out for human victims as an offering to Durga, attacked them. The prince fought bravely and a number of tribesmen were killed. But at last he was overpowered through the sheer weight of their numbers. Sundarasena and Dridhabuddhi were bound with ropes and carried to a prison. It was a dark cell, full of vermin and cobwebs, with snakes and scorpions crawling in and out. In this place they were amazed to see their two companions Bhimabhuja and Vikramashakti. The prince exclaimed, 'Alas, strange are the ways of fate. I desired with all my heart that I should see these friends of mine again.

My desire is granted; but where do I see them? In this hell, waiting to be executed!'

On the fourteenth day of the month, the bandits dragged the prisoners out of the cell and hauled them up before the image of Durga. The king of the Pulindas, Vindhyaketu, had already arrived to witness the ceremony. Now this king had often visited Alaka to pay homage to King Mahasena, whose overlordship was recognized by all the neighbouring kingdoms. Sundarasena recognized him but kept quiet.

Vindhyaketa said to one of his followers, 'Where is that human victim who put up such a brave fight against you? I am curious to see him.' Sundarasena was brought near Vindhyaketu. When the Pulinda Chief saw him he half recognized the prince and asked him who he was. Sundarasena said haughtily, "How does it matter to you where I come from? Go ahead with your ceremony and finish it as quickly as you can.' Vindhyaketu recognized him completely by his voice and said, 'Ah, wretch that I am! What benefits have I not received from King Mahasena? And how do I repay them? By ill-treating his son, and preparing to kill him.' He ordered his followers to release Sundarasena and his companions. He embraced the prince with great affection and conducted him to his mansion. After the prince and his friends had eaten their meal and rested, Vindhyaketu asked them how they happened to be in that forest. The prince narrated his adventures and Vindhyaketu heard them with great amazement.

Sundarasena's stars had now again begun to smile upon him. His bad days were over. No sooner had he narrated his adventures than a tribesman came running to the king of Pulindas and said, 'Oh King, a certain merchant was shipwrecked and we captured him along with a prodigious amount of wealth. The villain has in his possession a very beautiful lady. We have imprisoned them both, and they shall soon be brought into your presence.'

After a short while, Vindhyaketu's soldiers came with their captives. Imagine the joy and surprise of Sundarasena when he saw that the beautiful lady was none other than Princess Mandaravati! The merchant was given a sound thrashing. In a voice trembling with fear he said, 'Spare me, sinner though I am. It is true that I had evil intentions, but no harm has been done. This saintly lady has preserved her honour. She has kept me at a distance as though she were a blazing fire. When she repulsed me so violently, I decided to carry her to my own country and, after allaying her anger, to make her my wife.' Vindhyaketu wanted to execute the merchant on the spot. But Sundarasena intervened. The merchant's wealth was confiscated and he was driven into the forest.

Vindhyaketu paid all honour to Mandaravati. She was provided with new clothes and Pulinda women attended to her toilet. That evening the king gave a great banquet at which accomplished dancers and singers performed before the guests.

At Sundarasena's request the king of Pulindas despatched a messenger with a letter for King Mahasena. The messenger reached Alaka just when the king and queen, unable to endure their grief any longer, had decided to immolate themselves in a fire in front of the temple of Siva. When news of Sundarasena's safety was announced, the city of Alaka went wild with joy. The letter-carrier was loaded with gifts. Next day, impatient to meet his son, King Mahasena marched towards the land of the Pulindas, accompanied by the king of Hamsadvipa.

Sundarasena and Mandaravati met the king's party on the way. Great was their rejoicing when the two young people met their fathers again. Mandaravati touched the feet of her future father-in-law, and all those who watched the scene were inundated by waves of joy. Shortly after this the hour fixed by the astrologers arrived. The marriage of Sundarasena and Mandaravati was celebrated with unprecedented magnificence. King Mandaradeva returned to Hamsadvipa. King Mahendraditya who had proved such a faithful and loving ally, bestowed many presents on the newly wedded couple and returned to Shashankapura. And Vindhyaketu, the lord of the great wilderness, after apologizing to King Mahasena for the harshness he had unwittingly shown to his son, made his way back to the forest.

A few months later, King Mahasena, perceiving that his son was virtuous, and that the happiness of the subjects was safe in his hands, placed him on the throne and retired to the forest. Thus Sundarasena became the King of Alaka. With the help of his five faithful companions he subjugated all the kingdoms that his father had omitted to conquer. And for a long, long time he ruled over his mighty empire in the company of his beloved queen, Mandaravati.

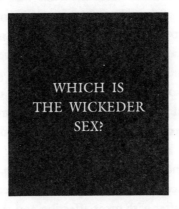

WHICH IS
THE WICKEDER
SEX?

In the city of Pataliputra there once lived a prince named Vikramakesarin. Providence had made him a treasure of virtues and he himself possessed a treasure of jewels. Now this prince had a parrot whom he loved very dearly. The name of this parrot was Vidaghachudamani. The extraordinary thing about him was that he knew all the *Shastras* and his intellect was as sharp as a razor. In fact his parrot existence was the temporary result of Indra's curse. He was actually a *Gandharava* named Chitraratha. For some fault or the other he was banished from his celestial home and sent to the earth as a parrot.

Prince Vikramakesarin consulted this wise bird in all important matters. In course of time the prince married, on the parrot's advice, a princess of the royal family of Magadha. The name of the princess was Chandraprabha. Now, as chance would have it, she possessed a *maina* named Somika who was the equal of the parrot in knowledge and wisdom. She, too, was once a denizen of the celestial regions. She was a nymph, and her real name was Tilottama. Owing to some transgression of rules she had been banished from heaven and condemned to live as a *maina* for a while.

Princess Chandraprabha brought the *maina* along with her to her husband's palace. The two birds were lodged in the same cage. They were looked after with great affection and they themselves never failed to give to the prince and the princess appropriate advice on all occasions.

One day the parrot said to the *maina:* 'My dear, we live in the same cage, perch on the same rod and share the same food. Why should we not get married? I am proposing to you. Will you accept me?'

To his surprise the *maina* turned him down unceremoniously. 'I have nothing against you', she said. 'But all males are wicked and ungrateful. I shall never allow myself to get involved in a permanent attachment with any member of that sex.'

The parrot was touched to the quick by this aspersion on the male sex. 'How dare you utter such a falsehood!' he said sharply. 'The fact is exactly the reverse. All females are cruel and faithless.'

And so a mighty dispute arose between them. When all their arguments and counter-arguments led to nothing, they decided to submit their case to the judgment of the prince. A bargain was made between them: should the parrot win his case, the *maina* was to become his wife; should he lose, he was to become her slave.

The prince agreed to act as the judge. The birds were invited to the royal judgment-hall and the issue between them was placed before the prince. The judge said to the *maina*, 'You assert that males are ungrateful. How do you support this statement?'

The *maina* said, 'Sir, I shall advance no arguments. I shall merely narrate a true story. On the basis of my story you can judge whether or not males are ungrateful wretches.'

And so she told the following story.

* * *

In the city of Kamandaki there was a rich merchant named Arthadatta. A son was born to him and was given the name of Dhanadatta. When he grew up Dhanadatta fell into evil company, and, on his father's death, began to squander the family property. He took to gambling and allowed himself to be surrounded by a set of rogues. Wicked society is the root from which grows the tree of sin. In the case of Dhanadatta the tree grew very rapidly. He soon ran through his father's treasure and, ashamed of his poverty, left his country to wander in foreign lands.

In the course of his travels he reached the prosperous city of Chandanapura where chance led him to the house of a merchant. In spite of his poverty and dissipation Dhanadatta still looked a presentable young man. The merchant took a fancy to him and admitted him to his household. Since the newcomer was of noble descent, and his demeanour was polished, the merchant bestowed upon him the hand of his daughter Ratnavali. He settled a dower upon his son-in-law and Dhanadatta began to live comfortably in his wife's house.

But he did not remain content with his new-found happiness. Being in possession of wealth once again, he longed for fresh pleasures and wanted to return to his own country. His father-in-law was unwilling to let him go, since Ratnavali was his only child. But Dhanadatta insisted so eagerly that the merchant had to agree. So the young man set out, accompanied by his wife and an old serving-maid.

Ratnavali was wearing expensive jewellery. As they were passing through a deep forest, the sight of his wife's ornaments stirred the villain in Dhanadatta. On the pretext that there was a danger of robbers, he persuaded his wife to part with her ornaments and make them over to him for safekeeping.

And now perceive, noble prince, how brutal and heartless the male sex can be. This villain, Dhanadatta, threw his innocent and virtuous wife into a ravine along with the old woman. And, having done this wicked deed, he went away chuckling at the thought of all the gems in his pocket.

The old woman was killed, but Ratnavali was caught in a tangled mass of creepers and her life was saved. Painfully she climbed out of the ravine, clinging to branches of trees growing on the mountain side. Groping in all directions she ultimately reached the main road and, with her limbs sorely bruised, returned to her father's house. Her parents were shocked to see her in that condition and anxiously asked what had befallen her.

And now perceive, noble prince, how generous and faithful a female can be. Poor Ratnavali, so outrageously treated by her husband, swallowed all her humiliation and never breathed a word about Dhanadatta's treachery.

'We were set upon by bandits,' she said. 'My husband was bound and taken away. The old woman and myself were thrown into a deep valley. Luckily for me I was dragged out of the ravine by a kindhearted traveller. The old woman died of her injuries but I managed to scramble back home. 'Her parents comforted her and she remained with them, thinking of her husband all the time.

Meanwhile Dhanadatta reached his home and resumed his former ways. He sold the ornaments that he had so deceitfully obtained from his wife and very soon his house became a gambling den. But the cash did not last long. Once more he found himself without a coin and, with incredible impudence, decided to revisit his father-in-law and secure more wealth. He reflected: 'The merchant is a simple-minded person. I shall tell him that I have left my wife at home. He will trust me. I can easily get round him and obtain a substantial sum of money.'

But when he approached his father-in-law's house whom should he see but his own wife! Dhanadatta was taken aback, but his wife came to him and fell at his feet. However wicked a husband might be, a good wife does not waver in her affection. Ratnavali told him the story that she had cooked for her parents. Dhanadatta was now emboldened and entered his father-in-law's house. The merchant embraced him fondly and said, 'My son, fate has been kind to us. You have escaped from the hands of the bandits without a scratch. Now remain here peacefully.'

But is there any limit to the wickedness of a male? For a few days Dhanadatta lived with Ratnavali, pretending to love her tenderly. And then, grasping his chance one dark night, he killed his wife while she slept upon his bosom. He grabbed all the ornaments that she was wearing and others that were kept in the jewel-box. Then, slipping out of the house unobserved, he hastened to his own city in order to indulge in fresh dissipations.

Such is the race of males. It is for you to judge, Oh Prince, whether my remarks were unjustified.

* * *

Prince Vikramakesarin, having heard the *maina's* story with great interest, turned to the parrot. 'My dear Vidagdhachudamani,' he said, 'you have heard Somika's presentation of the ease. Now what do you have to say?'

The parrot replied, 'Prince, I still maintain that all females are wicked and disloyal. Moreover, they are thoroughly immoral and given

to bodily carvings. Let me tell you a true story to prove this.'
And so the parrot narrated the following story.

* * *

There was once a merchant named Dharmadatta. He had a daughter
whose beauty was the talk of the city. Her name was Vasudatta. Her
father loved her dearly and found for her a young man worthy to be
her husband. The name of this young man was Samudradatta and he
lived in the city of Tamralipti, renowned for the honesty of its
inhabitants. Samudradatta was rich, virtuous and exceedingly
handsome. Lovely women gazed upon him as doves gaze upon the
moon.

For some time after their marriage Samudradatta and Vasudatta
lived happily together. But as soon as her husband went to his own
city on a visit, Vasudatta forgot her marriage-vows. Fickle and
unfaithful, as females generally are, she fixed her attention upon a
handsome young man who lived near her father's house. She invited
him through a go-between and very soon adopted him as her
paramour.

When the husband returned, Vasudatta's parents decorated the
house with great joy. They made her put on new clothes and jewels.
But the young woman was indifferent to her husband. When he spoke
to her she pretended to be asleep. And when, overcome by fatigue,
he was himself sunk in the oblivion of sleep, she made ready to slip
out of the house. At that very moment a thief entered the house and
watched her movements. The thief reflected: 'What a strange situation.
She has gone out at dead of night wearing those very jewels which I
had come to steal. There is something fishy here. Let me follow her
and see where she goes.' And so the thief kept an eye on her, following
her from a distance. She entered a garden outside the city and began
to look for her lover, with whom she had made a secret assignation.

But the lover had been surprised by the city guards, taken for a runaway thief, and put to death. His body dangled from a tree and there was a halter round his neck. Vasudatta was distracted, but only for a while. She lowered her paramour's body and, hoping that he might still be alive, adorned it with flowers and perfumes. Even though he was senseless she embraced him, so completely was her mind blinded by passion. Meanwhile a goblin had taken possession of the corpse and he suddenly bit off Vasudatta's nose. Convinced that her lover was indeed dead, and suffering great pain, she slowly made her way to her own apartment. The thief who had watched the entire sequence of events was shocked. 'Will woman's wickedness admit no limit!' he reflected. 'Black and dark like a well is the mind of a female. It is unfathomable. I wonder what she will do now.' And he followed her again, out of curiosity.

Vasudatta entered her own chamber where her husband was sleeping and started screaming, 'Help! help! This wicked husband of mine has crossed all limits of cruelty. Now he has cut off my nose, though I have done him no wrong. Save me, father! He will not hesitate to kill me.' Her cries awakened everybody in the house and her parents came rushing to the chamber, followed by servants and neighbours. Seeing that her nose had been chopped off, Vasudatta's father bound her husband with stout ropes. The poor man remained speechless and did not understand why every one had suddenly turned against him. In the midst of this confusion the thief quietly slipped away.

Dharmadatta had great influence with the king and demanded that the husband should be executed. The king looked into all the circumstances and ordered that the death sentence be carried out. The young man pleaded innocence but no one listened to his version of the story. As he was being led to the place of execution, the thief approached the officers and said, 'This man is innocent. I know the true circumstances. Take me to the King. I shall reveal the whole story.'

So they took him to the king and, after receiving a promise of pardon for his acts of thievery, he narrated the entire story. The king seemed to doubt his words. But the thief said, 'Your Majesty, if you do not believe me, please send your officers to the garden which I have mentioned. I am sure you will find this woman's nose in the corpse's mouth.' The king accepted the suggestion and the officers, after visiting the garden, confirmed the thief's version.

The king was incensed by the woman's wickedness, and ordered that her ears also should be cut off. She was then banished from the country, while the young man who had come very near death through her wickedness was not only acquitted honourably but was also given costly presents. And the thief, who had furthered the ends of justice, was appointed the Chief Magistrate of the city.

* * *

'So you see, noble prince,' said Vidagdhachudamani, 'that females are wicked and treacherous by nature. It is now for you to judge between me and Somika.'

Prince Vikramakesarin was unable to make up his mind. He was pondering over the two stories that he had heard, and trying to decide which of them had greater force, when Indra's curse expired and the parrot once more became the *Gandharva* Chitraratha. Assuming a heavenly form, he flew away into the unknown. At that very moment the *maina's* term of earthly existence also expired. The curse pronounced upon her ceased to be effective. Forthwith she became the heavenly nymph Tilottama and vanished from sight.

And so the dispute concerning the wickedness of the sexes remained undecided in the judgment-hall of Prince Vikramakesarin.

THE STORY OF KING
UDAYANA

No other part of our earth
has won greater renown than the country of Vatsa. God must have
created this region deliberately to humble the pride of heaven—so
beautiful, so glorious is it in every way.

The chief city of this land is Kaushambi, the favourite residence
of the goddess of plenty. Here, long ago, King Shatanika held his sway.
He came of the great Pandava family. He was the son of Janamejaya,
and traced his ancestry to the mighty Arjuna, whose valour was tested
in a struggle against Siva himself.

For many years King Shatanika and his wife, Vishnumati, bewailed the absence of progeny. One day the king, who was roaming in a forest in search of game, strayed into the hermitage of Shandilya. In the course of their conversation the king told the sage how earnestly he longed for a son. Moved by his unhappiness, Shandilya came to Kaushambi and prepared a potion for the queen. Mystic verses were recited as the queen sipped the medicine. Shandilya's efforts did not go in vain. Very soon a son was born to Shantanika and Vishnumati.

The boy was named Sahasranika. He grew into a fine lad and became an ornament to his father, as humility is an ornament to perfection. Sahasranika was proclaimed the Crown Prince and King Shatanika gradually prepared to withdraw himself from the cares of government.

But, when destiny wills otherwise, can any one find peace or leisure? A war broke out between the gods and demons. Indra sent an urgent message asking Shatanika to assist him in his hour of need. The king entrusted his son to the care of his minister, Yogandhara, and his commander-in-chief, Supratika. Then he hurried to the battlefield where, fighting bravely, he met with a hero's death. Vishnumati perished on her husband's pyre and Sahasranika became the ruler of Vatsa.

The war was over. The demons were routed. Sahasranika went to Indra's heavenly city to join the festivities in celebration of the victory. There he saw many wondrous sights, but none that stirred him more than the fair ones who sported in the garden of Indra. 'Ah!' he exclaimed, 'If only I could find a wife as lovely as one of these beauties.'

Perceiving his desire, Indra cheered him. 'My friend', he said, 'You have not the least reason to feel despondent. A maiden worthy to be your wife was born many years ago. Your bride-to-be is Mrigavati, daughter of King Kritavarman of Ayodhya. Her beauty will hold you spellbound.' With these words Indra bade him farewell and placed at his disposal his own chariot to convey him back from Heaven to earth. The chariot was steered by Indra's favourite driver, Matali. As Sahasranika set out from heaven, his heart was burning with love for the maiden whose charms Indra had described. When, therefore, a nymph called Tilottama spoke to him, just as he was about to leave, her tender words made no impression upon him. In fact he scarcely heard her, so entirely was he wrapped in the vision of his future wife. Tilottama angrily cursed him for his indifference. 'Very well, proud monarch!' she threatened, 'You will suffer for this. For a long period of fourteen years will you endure separation from this woman, this Mrigavati whose image has led you to slight me.' But even this imprecation was heard only by Matali. The king was so much absorbed in his thoughts that he did not hear a syllable.

As soon as the king returned to Kaushambi, he sent an ambassador to Ayodhya with a proposal of marriage between himself and Princess Mrigavati. King Kritavarman of Ayodhya, and his queen, Kalavati, received the message with unfeigned delight. The ambassador from Kaushambi was lavishly entertained. Mrigavati herself sang and danced at the reception. Acceptance of the proposal was announced without delay. Both kingdoms rejoiced as Sahasranika arid Mrigavati were united in matrimony.

Fortune seemed to smile upon Kaushambi. Not long after the king's marriage, his counsellors were blessed with sons. The sons of Yogandhara and Supratika were named, respectively, Yaugandharayana and Rumanvat. A son was also born to the Master of Revels. He was named Vasantaka. Finally, as if to crown the king's happiness, Mrigavati told him that she was expecting a child.

But the king's joy was destined to be short-lived. From the heights of contentment he was soon to dive into the depths of bitter sorrow. A great tragedy awaited him.

Mrigavati, as her pregnancy advanced, acquired strange longings.

Among other things, she craved for a bath in a tank filled with blood. The king was too righteous to permit destruction of any living creature to gratify such a whim. But he had a tank filled to the brim with the juice of lac and other red extracts. While the queen was bathing in the blood-red water, an eagle suddenly pounced upon her and carried her off, mistaking her for a lump of raw flesh. The king helplessly watched his beloved disappearing in the sky and, unable to bear the grief, he fell into a swoon.

Matali, the charioteer of Indra, divined what had come to pass. He visited Kaushambi and, when the king had somewhat recovered his senses, revealed the curse uttered by Tilottama. Sahasranika was plunged in gloom; but the hope of future reunion sustained him and he somehow turned his attention once again to affairs of state.

Meanwhile the eagle, discovering that his prey was alive, abandoned Mrigavati on the top of a mountain. Distracted with sorrow and fear, she longed for death. But death did not come her way. Even when she flung herself in front of a wild elephant, she remained unharmed. The mighty beast gently put her aside. An enormous serpent rose up and prepared to swallow her. But a heavenly hero mysteriously appeared from nowhere, slew the serpent, and vanished.

After some time a hermit's son happened to pass that way in search of roots and fruit. He heard the wailing and lamentation of the unhappy queen and, with words of consolation and good cheer, led her to the hermitage of Jamadagni. Here Mrigavati took up her abode and, when her time was due, gave birth to a charming son. As soon as the child was delivered a voice was heard from heaven: 'Let the universe rejoice! A great king has been born. He shall win splendid fame, and his name shall be Udayana.'

And so the boy was named Udayana. He grew up in the peaceful grove with no other playmates than his own wonderful talents. Jamadagni instructed him in all the sciences and he also became skilled in archery, as behoved a warrior's son. And with infinite affection Mrigavati drew from her arm the bracelet that bore the name of Sahasranika and placed it on her son's.

Once, roaming about in pursuit of deer, Udayana met a tribesman who had just captured a snake. Out of pity for the beautiful snake Udayana approached its captor and beseeched him to release the animal. The tribesman said, 'My lord, I am a poor man. I make my living by exhibiting dancing snakes. The snake that had served me thus far died recently. After searching long in the great forest I found this one and charmed him into submission. Please do not ask me to part with my source of livelihood.'

But Udayana was determined to see the snake set at liberty. He gave away his bracelet to the tribesman in exchange for the snake. As he was about to release the animal from bondage, and turn his footsteps homeward, the snake addressed him. 'I am Vasunemi, the elder brother of Vasuki, monarch of the serpent race. In return for your generosity I give you four gifts: a lute of remarkable sweetness, a betel leaf that has special qualities, the art of weaving garlands that never fade, and the art of making indelible marks on the forehead.'

Udayana received these gifts gratefully and returned to the hermitage of Jamadagni. His sight was like nectar to Mrigavati's eyes.

In the meantime the snake charmer wandered far and wide with his valuable acquisition. Eventually he reached a thriving market and tried to sell the bracelet. The royal mark on the ornament aroused suspicion. He was arrested by the police and hauled up before the king. Sahasranika questioned the man minutely and marvelled at the story he related. As he was fondly gazing at the bracelet that had once enhanced his beloved wife's charms a voice from heaven said: 'Oh King, the curse is at an end. Your wife Mrigavati is residing in the hermitage of Jamadagni, together with your son.' These words assuaged the king's misery as the first raindrops of July relieve the heat-afflicted peacocks.

He somehow passed that night, full of expectation, and the next morning set out with a chosen band of followers in the direction of the eastern mountain. The snake-charmer accompanied him and showed him the way.

In a few days Sahasranika reached the hermitage of Jamadagni on the eastern mountain. He met the sage, who looked like a graven image of piety. The arbour was so tranquil that even the deer had abandoned their friskiness. Here, at last, the king tasted the bliss of reunion with his long-lost wife. He saw for the first time his son, Udayana, and clasped him in a close embrace. For a long time his body was riveted to his son's, as if the hair which stood erect with joy had nailed them together.

The king bade a tender farewell to Jamadagni and set out for Kaushambi with Mrigavati and Udayana. The fawns of the *ashrama* followed them for many a mile with tearful eyes.

Diverting themselves on the way by describing their respective adventures during the period of separation, the king and queen approached their home. Kaushambi was decked out with banners and arches of welcome. When the royal party arrived, the citizens feasted their eyes upon their beloved king and queen, and upon the prince they had never seen.

Udayana was proclaimed as the Crown Prince and entrusted with more and more authority as days passed. The king led a life of leisure and ease in the company of Mrigavati. At last, when old age sent its grey messenger to the region of the king's temples, Udayana was installed upon the throne as the full-fledged sovereign. Sahasranika assigned to his son three worthy advisers—Rumanvat, Yaugandharayana and Vasantaka—whose fathers had served him faithfully and well. And then, having ensured the prosperity of his people, he ascended the Himalayas, accompanied by Mrigavati, to prepare for the last journey.

The kingdom of Vatsa prospered. Kaushambi became the envy

of the world. Udayana ruled his subjects wisely and justly. But he had one weakness which caused his counsellors great anxiety: he was excessively fond of hunting. When engaged in a chase he would forget everything else in the world. He developed a particular fondness for trapping and subduing wild elephants. Being an accomplished musician, Udayana made good use of the lute which the serpent Vasunemi had given him in his boyhood. The dulcet notes which Udayana cajoled out of this lute cast a spell on infuriated elephants. They became tame and submissive. Overpowering them while in this state, the king brought back to his capital these mighty beasts of the forest.

Many years passed. Udayana, now in the prime of manhood, looked about him for a suitable wife. Vasavadatta, the daughter of Chandamahasena, king of Ujjayini, was reputed for her beauty and grace. Her charms were described to the king by so many people, and in such glowing terms, that he acquired a deep longing for the princess. But how could he obtain her hand? Ujjayini and Kaushambi were traditional enemies and Udayana hesitated to make a proposal that was in danger of being discourteously received.

Meanwhile, Chandamahasena himself had marked out Udayana as the most suitable husband he could find for his daughter. He knew the advantages of such an alliance; the combined power of Ujjayini and Kaushambi would be invincible. He made up his mind to employ every stratagem necessary to bring about the marriage. To begin with, he sent a message to Udayana extolling his skill in music and requesting him to come over to Ujjayini and initiate Vasavadatta in the art.

Udayana was justly furious at this presumptuous message. He summoned his minister, Yaugandharayana, and said, 'My friend, here is a message from Chandamahasena. I fail to understand his purpose in sending such an impudent proposal. Has any one ever heard of a monarch accepting a tutorship in an alien kingdom? What does the villain mean by this?' Yaugandharayana said, 'Your Majesty, I shall speak my mind plainly. This is what comes of acquiring a reputation for kingly vices. Evidently the king of Ujjayini has heard of your passion for music and your interminable hunting expeditions. He has judged you as a person who cannot resist his impulses. And so he hopes to ensnare you by the charms of his daughter. Kings should not be under the influence of strong passions. Otherwise they are captured by their enemies, even as wild elephants are taken in pits!'

The king did not feel offended by his minister's plain words. He knew that they proceeded from an affectionate regard for his true interests. The very next day he sent an ambassador to Chandamahasena with the message: 'If your daughter wishes to be my pupil, let her come to Kaushambi. I shall find some time to teach her.'

Udayana's anger did not abate even after the message, was despatched. He declared that he would march against Ujjayni and bring Chandamahasena back in chains. Yaugandharayana restrained him. He said, 'Sir, this is not the right course. Nor is it in your power to adopt it with any degree of success. Chandamahasena is a mighty monarch. Perhaps you are not familiar with his prowess. Let me tell you about it.'

And then Yaugandharayana related the history of Chandamahasena's valorous deeds.

'You have already heard about Ujjayini,' said Yaugandharayana, 'the mighty city that boasts of a thousand palaces. Now this wonderful city of Ujjayini was once ruled by King Mahendravarman. He conquered many lands and bequeathed to his son, Jayasena, a kingdom that became the envy of all the monarchs in the world. To Jayasena was born a son who was named Mahasena. He grew up into a hero of stupendous strength.

When Mahasena ascended the throne he said: 'I now want two things truly worthy of me—a sword such as no hero has ever wielded, and a wife who combines all perfections in herself.' With this thought came the determination to undergo stern austerities in order to win these gifts from the gods. Mahasena went to the temple of Durga and propitiated the goddess through self-mortification. He remained without food and water for a long period and even cut off pieces of his own flesh as an offering to the deity.

Gratified by his devotion, the goddess appeared in visible form and said, 'My son, I am touched by your steadfastness. Your longings shall be fulfilled. Here is a sword that will make you invincible. Take it and perform heroic deeds. As for your second wish, you must know that your bride-to-be is Angaravati, the daughter of a powerful demon named Angaraka. She is the most beautiful maiden in the three worlds. You will be proud of her. Go back to Ujjayini now. And in commemoration of the cruel penance that you have performed, you will henceforward be called Chandamahasena.'

That is how Mahasena became Chandamahasena. Armed with his invincible sword, he vanquished all enemies. And his power was further increased when he came in possession of a fighting elephant named Nadagiri. Never was a more redoubtable elephant seen on a battlefield. At the mere sight of Nadagiri all other elephants fled in terror.

One day he saw in a forest an enormous wild boar. Its aspect was terrible. The blackness of a dark night seemed to be congealed into the solid body of that ferocious animal. Chandamahasena riddled the boar with arrows but it was none the worse for them. It boldly approached the king's chariot, smashed it into pieces, and disappeared into a cavern.

Intent upon vengeance, the king entered the deep cavern with only his bow to defend himself with. After he had travelled a long while through the gloomy cave, he suddenly came upon a splendid city. In the middle of the city there was a lake. And on the bank of the lake he saw a maiden of wondrous beauty. Her glance was like the arrow of love which cleaves the shield of self restraint. The king was completely captivated by her charms and she, in her turn, gazed upon him with eyes full of tenderness.

Slowly she walked up to the king and asked, 'Noble Sir, what is your august name? And what has prompted you to visit our home?' When he told that he had come in pursuit of a wild boar, she gave expression to bitter anxiety. 'Alas, you are lost!' she exclaimed. 'The boar that you have been pursuing is only an assumed form of the demon, Angaraka. I am his daughter and I know how ruthless he is. These maidens you see around me have all been carried off by him from the palaces of mighty kings. He has imprisoned them here as servants to wait upon me. At the moment he has discarded his animal guise and is resting in his true form. But as soon as he wakes up he will do you injury.' With these words the maiden burst into tears; for Angaravati, the daughter of Angaraka, was already in love with the king.

Chandamahasena kept his presence of mind and said, 'Oh lovely maiden, if you wish me well do what I tell you and ask no questions. As soon as your father wakes up you must go near him and pretend to weep. When he asks you the reason of your agitation you must say, 'Dearest father, if some one were to slay you how could 1 bear to live? This thought is the cause of my grief.''

Angaravati did as she was told. When the demon heard the reason of her anxiety he burst into laughter. 'What a foolish child you are, my dear,' he said. 'How can any one possibly slay me? My entire body is protected by a shield that nothing can pierce. There is only one unguarded spot in my left arm, but that is always concealed by my bow.'

Chandamahasena heard this revelation from his place of concealment. He bided his time, and as soon as the demon rose from his bath the king insolently challenged him to a fight. Angaraka was preparing for his daily worship of Siva. So he raised his left arm and made a gesture asking the king to wait for a few moments.

Chandamahasena grasped his opportunity and smote the demon at the vulnerable spot. With a piercing cry Angaraka collapsed and lay dead on the ground. The king took his daughter as his prize and returned to Ujjayini

The marriage of Chandamahasena and Angaravati was celebrated with great pomp. After a few years two sons were born to them. The first was called Gopalaka and the second, Palaka. A great feast was held in honour of Indra. The same night Indra came to the king in a dream and said: 'I am pleased by the reverence you have shown me. By my favour you will soon obtain a daughter of matchless beauty.'

In course of time the king was indeed blessed with a graceful daughter. When she was born, people thought that the creator was no longer content with one moon in the firmament and desired another on earth. And, since the gift was born through the blessing of Indra, who is also known as 'Vasava', the King named her Vasavadatta, 'Given by Vasava'.'

* * *

This is how Yaugandharayana narrated the history of Chandamahasena. After a while he addressed King Udayana again. 'You will thus see,' he said, 'that the king of Ujjayini is not to be trifled with. His power is immense and his capital city is situated in a difficult terrain. Nevertheless, you must not give up the hope of marrying Vasavadatta. She remains in the house of her father as Lakshmi, the Goddess of Prosperity, remained in the gloomy depths of the ocean before it was churned. Moreover Chandamahasena is himself eager to give his daughter to you. Only, being a proud monarch, he wants to do so with a show of triumph.'

When he heard these words Udayana became even more enamoured of beautiful Vasavadatta.

Meanwhile the ambassador from Vatsa travelled to Ujjayini and delivered his master's reply. When Chandmahasena heard the message he reflected: 'Well, I was too simple to expect that the king of Vatsa could be so easily persuaded to come here. He will never agree. And of course I cannot send Vasavadatta to Kaushambi. That would be unbecoming. I must think of some clever stratagem to imprison him.'

Ultimately the king, in consultation with his ministers, hit upon an unusual plan. He ordered skilled craftsmen to manufacture an artificial elephant. When it was ready and he was satisfied that it was sufficiently lifelike, he placed his bravest warriors inside the contraption and had it conveyed to a remote part of the Vindhya forest.

Udayana soon heard from his guards that an exceptionally large elephant was seen on the outskirts of his kingdom. He was tempted by the prospect of a splendid hunt. He also thought that, if the elephant was really as fantastically large as the guards claimed, it might well serve as a rival to Nadagiri. By capturing it alive he hoped to neutralize Chandamahasena's advantage.

And so, disregarding the warning of his court astrologers, Udayana set out for the Vindhya forest. On the southern slope he saw an elephant of truly magnificent appearance. Through fear of alarming it, the king made his companions halt at a distance and advanced alone. He approached the elephant slowly, playing a soft melody on his lute. Evening shadows were thickening and Udayana was completely deceived. The elephant flapped its ears, as if enraptured by the music, while it approached and retreated by turns. When the king was drawn deep into the forest, the warriors suddenly emerged from their place of concealment. Udayana was armed only with a hunting knife. Resistance was useless. He was overpowered and carried off to Ujjayini.

Chandamahasena came out to meet his royal captive and conveyed him to the palace with utmost respect. The citizens of Ujjayini saw the king of Vatsa with great admiration. He was like the moon—beautiful, but stained with defeat. Hearing that Udayana would be put to death, many of the citizens announced that they would commit suicide in protest. Chandamahasena calmed the agitation by publicly dispelling all rumours about Udayana's impending execution.

In the concert-hall of the royal palace, Vasavadatta was introduced to Udayana as a pupil eager to learn the art of music. As soon as she saw him her heart was steeped in love. Her eyes were averted through modesty, but her mind was fastened to the royal visage of the instructor. The king of Vatsa, in his turn, was overwhelmed by Vasavadatta's loveliness. His anger melted away. In his lap was the magic lute, in his throat the unsung melody, and before him was Vasavadatta, the delight of his heart.

The guards who had accompanied Udayana to the Vindhya forest returned to Kaushambi and broke the news of the king's captivity. The enraged citizens called for an immediate assault on Ujjayini. But Rumanvat, the wise and trusted general, checked their impetuosity. He reminded them that Chandamahasena was a powerful monarch and to attack him would mean endangering the very life of Udayana.

The three counsellors, Rumanvat, Yaugandharayana and Vasantaka, held a secret conference. After careful deliberation they adopted the plan which Yaugandharayana put forward. He said, 'Friends, the country is loyal to our king. Nevertheless, it is necessary that the commander-in-chief should stay here to guard the city. You must remain alert. When the right moment comes you will be called upon to show your prowess. I shall go to Ujjayini, accompanied only by Vasantaka. I know spells for breaking through walls and rending fetters. And I can count upon King Udayana's shrewdness. His wisdom shines forth in adversity, just as the flash of lightning is particularly brilliant during a storm.'

Thus, having entrusted to Rumanvat the care of the city, the wise minister set out with Vasantaka. He first visited Pulindaka, who ruled a kingdom in the hilly region of the Vindhyas. Yaugandharayana won him over and asked him to keep in readiness so that Udayana might find the necessary protection immediately after his flight from Ujjayini. The two friends next visited Mahakala, the dreadful burning-ground near Ujjayini, where they mastered many strange and unearthly charms. Approaching the palace of Chandamahasena, Yaugandharayana made good use of his newly acquired knowledge of spells. He transformed the appearance of Vasantaka as well as his own. Vasantaka now became an ugly buffoon with a large stomach and projecting teeth, while he himself assumed the form of an old, deformed hunchback. In these strange guises they soon attracted the curiosity of the townsfolk. With a crowd of jeering urchins at their heels, they reached the palace-gate. The women in the inner apartments, always on the lookout for some fresh source of diversion, saw from their balconies the antics of the hunchback and the clown. They described the spectacle to Vasavadatta.

Youth is twin brother to mirth. As soon as Vasavadatta came to know of this fun that was going on outside the walls of the palace, she sent a maid and ordered the strange visitors to be brought into the concert-room.

Yaugandharayana saw the king of Vatsa in fetters and burst into tears. However, he quickly mastered his grief and made a sign which Udayana immediately understood. Then Yaugandharayana, by means of his magic power, made himself invisible to Vasavadatta and her maids. Vasavadatta exclaimed in astonishment, 'Why, the madcap has vanished! Where could he have escaped?' Since Udayana continued to see his friend quite clearly, he grasped the situation. 'Go, my good girl,' he said gravely to Vasavadatta. 'Bring the requisites for the worship of Sarasvati so that we might resume the music-lesson.' As soon as she was out of the hall Yaugandharayana taught the king a spell for breaking chains. He also attached a charm to the strings of his lute so that Vasavadatta might become entirely submissive to his will.

And, having done his work, the devoted minister slipped out of the palace unnoticed.

Day by day Vasavadatta felt ever more deeply attached to Udayana. Yaugandharayana saw that the time was ripe for taking the decisive step. He found an opportunity to speak to the king in absolute privacy. And he outlined his plan in detail. 'Listen carefully, Your Majesty,' he said. 'Although Chandamahasena has made you captive by a mean artifice, he intends to bestow his daughter on you and to set you at liberty. We must forestall him and carry off his daughter. In this way we shall revenge ourselves upon him and the world will not think lightly of us.'

But how could such a daring project be executed? The idea of kidnapping, without the backing of an army, Ujjayini's royal princess seemed absurd. Yaugandharayana, however, had worked it all out. 'I have ascertained,' he said, 'that Vasavadatta has a remarkably swift female elephant named Bhadravati. The only elephant capable of overtaking her is Nadagiri; but he will not fight against her! The *mahout* in charge of Bhadravati has already been won over. He is our man. All you have to do is to ensure the silence of the Superintendent of Royal Elephants. This you can easily achieve through Vasavadatta's help. The rest is easy. You can escape at midnight and I shall make sure that the road you take is guarded by our new ally, Pulindaka.'

Udayana confided the plan to Vasavadatta. She readily threw in her lot with her future husband. On the pretext of offering oblations to the gods, Vasavadatta got a supply of syrups to which wine was generously added. After a ceremonial feast the Superintendent of the Royal Elephants, along with his staff, was treated to these intoxicating drinks.

In the silence of the night the king of Vatsa, accompanied by Vasavadatta and her companion Kanchanmala, mounted Bhadravati and left the palace. The gates were barred. But Bhadravati, with one mighty blow, battered down one of the ramparts. The guards outside were slain when they resisted. In the morning, the news of Udayana's escape was made known to Chandamahasena. He ordered his son, Palaka, to pursue the fugitives. Mounted on Nadagiri, Palaka succeeded in overtaking them; but at the sight of Bhadravati, Nadagiri refused to fight. Palaka had to return to Ujjayini and Udayana advanced towards the Vindhya forest.

Many adventures befell the party in the Vindhya forest. Bhadravati, who had served them so faithfully, died after drinking the polluted water of a wayside pond. Later, Udayana was attacked by brigands; but with unparalleled courage he fought and defeated them single-handed. At last they reached the plateau where Pulindaka, the tribal chieftain, was waiting for them. Rumanvat, the steadfast general, came from Kaushambi and joined his sovereign with a picked army of warriors.

Vasavadatta, fatigued after the difficult journey and depressed at having abandoned her parents and brothers, came close to Udayana and whispered to him words of tender love. She was bashful as well as impatient, and contrary feelings stirred her heart. Soon, however, she felt cheered by the news that her father, reconciling himself to the turn of events, was sending a message of friendship and goodwill to Udayana. This news was brought by a merchant who announced that the king's envoy had already set out from Ujjayini.

Udayana and Vasavadatta spent a few days as the guests of Pulindaka. Their anxiety was over. They were among friends and followers. They breathed with delight the pure air of the Vindhya mountains. And when Vasavadatta felt the need of diversion, Vasantaka regaled her with stories of strange events and beautiful things.

Very soon the messenger from Ujjayini reached the Vindhya forest and delivered this message from King Chandamahasena: 'My son, I do not blame you for carrying my daughter away. I wanted to give

Vasavadatta to you myself; but I abstained because, while you were a prisoner at Ujjayini, you would have taken the proposal in ill part. Now I only ask you to wait for a little while so that the marriage of my daughter might be celebrated with due attention to ritual. I am sending my son, Gopalaka, to your court. He will make the arrangements on my behalf.'

The king of Vatsa was now eager to return home. He asked his host, Pulindaka, to await the arrival of Prince Gopalaka. Then, seated on a gorgeous elephant with Vasavadatta by his side, he set out for Kaushambi. The army followed him. The clatter of arms and the sound of horses' hoofs seemed to proclaim the glory of Udayana to high heaven. Indeed, when clouds of dust soared skyward, mighty Indra was disturbed. He thought the mountains of earth were invading his home.

Udayana and Vasavadatta spent a night in a country castle that belonged to Rumanvat. Then, to the great delight of his beloved subjects, the king entered the capital. The city of Kaushambi waited for him bathed and resplendent, like a wife eager to welcome her husband after a long sojourn in far-off lands. Banners waved joyously and music filled the air. Lovely faces peered from the balconies of towering mansions, like golden lotuses blooming in the heavenly Ganga.

Vasavadatta's joy was complete when Gopalaka arrived. Tears dimmed her eyes as she looked at her brother. Next day, with due observance of prescribed ceremonies, Udayana received the hand of Vasavadatta, like a beautiful shoot newly budded on the creeper of love. As she walked round the sacrificial fire, smoke reddened her eyes. She was getting foretaste of the intoxication in store for her in her husband's chamber.

The treasury was filled with the jewels presented by kings of distant countries. Udayana conferred upon the assembled sovereigns distinctions appropriate to their status. Gopalaka and Pulindaka were invested with turbans of honour. The faithful counsellors, Yaugandharayana, Rumanvat and Vasantaka, received the reward which they deemed of greater value than wealth or honour—the affection and gratitude of their royal friend.

And so King Udayana, after many tribulations, was united with the adorable Vasavadatta, with whom he trod the path of happiness for a long, long time.

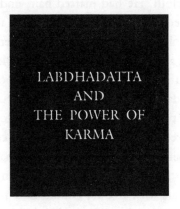

LABDHADATTA
AND
THE POWER OF
KARMA

In the city of Lakshapura there
once reigned a king named Lakshadatta. Never was a more generous
monarch heard of. When a suppliant merely came and stood in his
presence, he received a hundred thousand coins. But if he actually
conversed with the king, he received five hundred thousand. In fact it
was just because he never gave less than a lakh of coins that he was
called Lakshadatta.

And yet, strange to relate, there was a certain poor man named
Labdhadatta who never received a single copper from the king,
although he always remained at the palace gate. Poor Labdhadatta wore

only a ragged loincloth. He had matted hair; undernourishment had made him emaciated; and he did not possess a thing in the world. Day and night, in cold and in heat, in rainy weather and in dry weather he always remained at the gate, looking the very picture of misery. But the king never felt the desire to pull him out of poverty. And this was so because Labdhadatta's luck 'had not yet turned. The effects of his actions in past lives pursued him. Living so close to the most generous king on earth, he remained untouched by royal charity.

One day the king went on a hunt and Labdhadatta followed him, armed only with a stick. While the king, seated on a mighty elephant, killed tigers and bears with arrows, Labdhadatta played havoc among the wild beasts with his stick and despatched many of them. The king saw his courage and admired him, but gave him nothing. When the hunt was over, the king returned to his palace and resumed his diversions, while poor Labdhadatta stood at the gate as before.

On another occasion King Lakshadatta fell out with a neighbouring ruler. In the battle that followed Labdhadatta again displayed superhuman courage. Alone, and on foot, he struck down enemy after enemy with his wooden staff. The king watched his valour from his royal chariot and admired him. But he did not feel impelled to reward him with a single coin. When the dust of battle had settled they both returned to the city—the king to his luxurious chamber, and Labdhadatta to his wonted place outside the gate.

In this way five years came and went. Life in the palace went on as before, and Labdhadatta remained outside the gate growing thinner and looking more wretched every day. At last one day King Lakshadatta happened to see him and felt pity. 'This poor man has long remained miserable outside my palace,' he reflected. 'But I have never felt impelled to give him anything. This must be the result of his past deeds. Now let me find out whether fortune is ready to smile upon him.'

So the next day King Lakshadatta picked out some of the costly jewels from his treasury and placed them inside a melon that had been hollowed out. Then he summoned Labdhadatta and, in the presence of all his courtiers and ministers, said to him: 'My dear fellow, I often see you outside my palace gate. Why don't you recite some poem for me?' Labdhadatta promptly recited a couplet which he had composed. The purport of the lines was this: 'As the rivers replenish the sea, so do the streams of fortune replenish a man already rich. But they never come within the range of a poor man's eyes.'

The king praised the couplet very highly and with great ceremony presented the melon to Labdhadatta. At this all the courtiers were surprised. 'Who can fathom the ways of destiny?' they whispered. 'Here is a man with whom the king is pleased; and all that he gets is a melon. Indeed, for an unlucky person even the wishing-tree of paradise becomes a fig tree.'

Labdhadatta went out in a state of dejection. He happened to come across a mendicant who took a fancy to the fresh melon in his hand and obtained it from him in exchange for a garment. Ladbhadatta sold the garment and with the few coins that it fetched had a reasonably satisfying meal. On the next day he was back at his old place outside the palace. Meanwhile the mendicant went inside the palace and presented the fruit to the king. The king asked him, 'Sir, where did you get this melon?' And the mendicant said, 'Your Majesty, I got it from a man who habitually sits outside your palace.' When King Lakshadatta heard this he was convinced that Labdhadatta's fortune had not yet turned.

The next day the poor man was summoned again. He recited the same couplet and the king again gave him the same melon with great show of admiration. Without seeing what was inside the fruit, Labdhadatta gave it away to an official; and the official, in this turn, offered it to the king. On the third day Labdhadatta was again given the same fruit. This time he handed it over to one of the king's concubines who restored it to the king.

On the fourth day, however, when Labdhadatta was again made to recite his couplet, and was given the melon as a gift, the joining with which the fruit had been kept together broke. The jewels rolled out and the entire chamber was illuminated by their lustre. The courtiers whispered: 'Ah, how erroneous was our impression. We did not know the real situation and thought that the king was being ungracious.' And King Lakshadatta addressed them in these words: 'Gentlemen, you have seen how powerful is the effect of *karma*. By this artifice I merely wanted to find out whether fortune intended to lift this man out of poverty. As you all saw, although I gave him a veritable treasure he was not destined to enjoy it. Only today has the effect of his actions in past lives come to an end. And so his luck has turned.'

With these words the king loaded Labdhadatta with additional gifts and settled on him the revenue of a hundred villages.

GLOSSARY

Agni: *(i)* Fire, particularly altar-fire; *(ii)* A Vedic deity regarded as guardian of the sacred rites associated with fire.

Amrita: *(i)* Immortality; *(ii)* The nectar that bestows immortality.

Ananda: *(i)* Bliss; *(ii)* Name of the Buddha's closest disciple.

Apsaras: A celestial nymph.

Ashrama: A hermitage.

Asoka: Literally, 'free from sorrow'. *(i)* A much-prized Indian tree *(Saraca indica)* bearing bright, red flowers; *(ii)* Name of the famous emperor who ruled from 273 B.C. to 236 B.C. and was a great patron of Buddhism.

Bel: A tree *(Aegle marmelos)* which yields a large fruit of medicinal value.

Bhil: Member of a much-dreaded savage tribe.

Bodhisattva: Literally, 'He whose essence is Enlightenment'. The Buddha in one of his past or future incarnations.

Brahma: First of the Divine Triad (Brahma-Vishnu-Siva). The supreme deity in the aspect of Creator.

Brahman: The Impersonal Absolute of monistic metaphysics.

Brahmin: (i) A member of the highest caste; (ii) A priest.

Buddhas: (i) Enlightened beings; (ii) Liberated beings in Buddhist mythology.

The Buddha: The historical person, Shakyamuni Gautama, who founded the Buddhist faith. *(See* also 'Enlightened One'.)

Chakravaka: A bird which figures prominently in Sanskrit poetry, probably the shelldrake.

Chanakya: The author of the *Arthasastra,* the famous treatise on Political Economy and Diplomacy. *(See* also Kautilya.)

Chandala: A man of the lowest and most despised stratum of society.

Chataka: A bird who is said to subsist only on the first drops of rain every year, for which he patiently endures thirst for the remainder of the year.

Chitragupta: The recorder of human actions in Yama's realm. *(See* also Yama.)

Devadatta: The Buddha's wicked cousin, whose jealousy and hostility pursued him in all his incarnations.

Dhak: Also known as *Palasha,* a tree with showy red flowers. *(Butea frondosa* or 'Flame of the Forest'.)

Durga: A goddess, usually represented as terror-inspiring, associated with esoteric rites.

'Enlightened One': One of the epithets applied to the Buddha.

Gandharva: Member of a celestial race of musicians.

Garuda: (*i*) King of the birds; (*ii*) A fabulous bird serving as the vehicle of Vishnu.

'Great Being': One of the epithets frequently applied to the Bodhisattva.

Guru: Literally, 'weighty' or 'great'. A revered teacher or elder relative.

Harischandra: A legendary king, famed for his unswerving devotion to truth.

Indra: (*i*) King of the gods. (*ii*) The god of rain. (*See* also Vasava.)

Jain: A follower of the heterodox religion founded by Mahavira.

Jamadagni: Name of a famous *rishi*.

Jambu: Popular name, *jamun*. The rose-apple tree.

Jataka: Literally, 'Nativity'. A story, usually didactic, connected with one of the Buddha's former births.

Jetavana: A large park, so called because it was purchased from Prince Jeta by a lay disciple, where the Buddha often spent several weeks at a stretch.

Kailasa: A peak in the Himalayas, supposed to be the home of Siva.

Karma: (*i*) One's deeds or actions performed in lives past and present; (*ii*) One's inexorable destiny as determined by one's actions.

Kartika: A month corresponding roughly to October-November.

Kartikeya: The God of War, also known as Skanda.

Kashi: Traditional name for the city of Banaras. (See also Varanasi.)

Kautilya: Another name of Chanakya. (*See* also Chanakya.)

Kaveri: A well-known river in the extreme south of India.

Khajuraho: Site of the renowned eleventh–century temples with rich carvings.

Kinnara: Member of a race of mythical beings usually regarded as half-animal and half-human.

Kosala: Name of a region in northern India, once an important kingdom.

Kshatriya: A member of the warrior caste.

Kubera: The God of Riches.

Lakshmi: Wife of Vishnu, worshipped as the goddess of prosperity.

Lanka: Another name of Simhala (Ceylon). Sometimes the word Lanka indicates only the capital city of Ceylon. *(See* also Simhala.*)*

Magadha: Name of a kingdom in eastern India, at one time a great centre of political power and a seat of culture.

Mahout: Elephant-driver.

Maina: A small, black bird of the passerine order, noted for its capacity to imitate human speech.

Meru: A fabulous golden mountain around which the planets are supposed to revolve.

Mimamsa: An orthodox system of philosophy closely adhering to scriptural texts.

Moggallana: One of the favourite disciples of the Buddha.

Naga: (i) A snake; *(ii)* A legendary being with human face and serpentine body.

Narayana: A name of Vishnu. *(See* also Vishnu.)

Nyaya: (i) Justice, rectitude, propriety; *(ii)* An orthodox system of philosophy mainly concerned with logic.

Ocean-churning: The reference is to the myth according to which the gods and the demons churned the primeval ocean of milk, with Mount Meru as the churning rod and the snake, Vasuki, as the rope. The Ocean-churning is supposed to have yielded a number of precious objects, the last of which was a jar of nectar. (*See* also Parijata, Vasuki.)

Pali: A language, closely allied to Sanskrit, in which the canonical literature of Buddhism is preserved.

Panchatantra: Literally, 'Five Underlying Principles' or 'Five Doctrines'.

Pandavas: Heroes of the *Mahabharata* war, representing 'the Good' while Kauravas represented 'the Evil'.

Parijata: One of the mythical trees yielded up during Ocean churning. (*See* also Ocean-churning.)

Parvati: Daughter of the Himalayas and consort of Siva.

Pataliputra: The capital city of Magadha, associated with the names of many great emperors.

Pisacha: A demon or ghoul.

Prajapati: (*i*) Lord of all living creatures; (*ii*) A Vedic god at one time regarded as supreme.

Pulinda: Member of a wild mountain tribe.

Rakshasa: A nocturnal fiend.

Rama or Ramachandra: Prince of Ayodhya, hero of the epic poem *Ramayana*.

Ravana: The demon king of Lanka who was the adversary of Rama in the war described in the *Ramayana*. (*See* also Vibhishana.)

Rishi: A sage, a seer.

Sal: A large tree *(Shorea robusta)* frequently mentioned in Buddhist literature.

Sarasvati: (*i*) Name of a sacred river; (*ii*) Goddess of Speech, Learning and the Muses.

Sariputta: A favourite disciple of the Buddha.

Savatthi or Sravasti: A town where the Buddha delivered some of his most important sermons.

Shabara: Member of a wild tribe inhabiting the foothills.

Shastra: Scripture, canonical work.

Shravana: A month, corresponding to July-August, marked by heavy rainfall.

Shudra: A member of the menial caste.

Simhala: Another name for Ceylon. (*See* also Lanka.)

Siva: (*i*) Gracious, good, auspicious; (*ii*) Third in the Divine Triad (Brahma-Vishnu-Siva), sometimes also worshipped as the Supreme Being.

Stupa: A mound or other structure built over the relies of the Buddha or other leaders of the Buddhist church.

Takshashila: A city in north-western India, once a great center of learning.

Tamala: A tree *(Cinnamomum tamala)* with large, fragrant leaves.

Tathagata: Literally, 'He who has thus arrived'. A title of the Buddha.

Tilottama: Name of a heavenly nymph.

Vaishya: A member of the trading community.

Varanasi: The ancient name of Banaras. In recent years the name has been revived. (*See* also Kashi.)

Varuna: A Vedic god, the presiding deity of the Night, the West, and the Waters, often associated with Indra.

Vasava: A name of Indra. *(See* also Indra.)

Vasuki: (*i*)Sovereign of the serpents; (*ii*) The mythical serpent used as a rope in Ocean-churning. (*See* also Ocean-churning.)

Veena: The lute.

Vibhishana: The brother of Ravana, installed on the throne of Lanka by Ramachandra.

Vidarbha: A region south of the Vindhya mountain, once a prosperous kingdom.

Vidyadhara: Member of a tribe of celestial beings possessing knowledge of magical spells. The Vidyadharas are supposed to be attendants of Siva.

Vindhya: A mountain range running from east to west and roughly separating northern India from the Deccan.

Vishnu: Second of the Divine Triad (Brahma-Vishnu-Siva); the husband of Lakshmi; the Supreme Being in the aspect of Preserver.

Vyasa: Name of a great sage, the author of the *Mahabharata.*

Yajnavalkya: Name of a well-known sage and philosopher.

Yaksha: Member of a class of demigods in the service of Kubera, the God of Wealth.

Yama: (*i*) The God of Death: (*ii*) The Lord of the Nether Regions; (*iii*) The Supreme Punisher. (*See* also Chitragupta.)